GRYPHON BOOKS

8

Nancekuke

GRYPHON BOOKS
General Editor Rhodri Jones

John Branfield

Nancekuke

JOHN MURRAY

© John Branfield 1972

Published in *Gryphon Books* 1988 by
John Murray (Publishers) Ltd
50 Albemarle Street
London W1X 4BD

British Library Cataloguing in Publication Data

Branfield, John
  Nancekuke. — (Gryphon books; no. 8).
  I. Title   II. Series
  823′.914[F] PR6052.R27/

  ISBN 0-7195-4514-8

Typeset in 10/12pt Sabon
by Inforum Ltd, Portsmouth
Printed and bound in Great Britain
by Biddles of Guildford

Contents

Author's Note

This book is dedicated to my daughter, Susan. I wrote it from an idea we worked out together when she was very concerned – like many others – about Nancekuke. This was a chemical defence experimental establishment of the Ministry of Defence. It was on the north coast of Cornwall, close to where we live, between Newquay and St Ives.

We first knew what went on there when the papers gave publicity to a man who worked there and who claimed to be suffering from nerve gas poisoning. Other cases were mentioned, including some men who had died. The Ministry of Defence denied any connection between their illness and their work.

We tried to imagine what would happen to a family where the father had died in these circumstances. We made up a story about a girl whose father had worked at Nancekuke. This man – his research work, his visit to Germany, his illness – was our invention; he bore no resemblance as far as I know to anyone who had ever worked at Nancekuke, although his illness was like that of the former workers at Nancekuke whose cases were reported in the press.

But if the characters were all imaginary, the background to the book was factual. At that time Nancekuke produced CS gas and experimental quantities of nerve gas. Men who worked there fell ill with symptoms similar to those of nerve gas poisoning. Seals died in unexplained ways and in unusually large numbers. People who objected to research into chemical warfare, or to the siting of the factory, or to what they believed were its possible dangers, organized protests and demonstrations.

It was against the background of these facts that we set our story. I felt that there was a need for novels for and about young people, with contemporary settings and about real issues and I think that it is still true. This places a heavy responsibility upon the author and I took every possible care to make sure that documentary material was as correct as I was able to make it, according to information available at the time of writing.

Since then Nancekuke has ceased to be an experimental centre. It closed because of an international agreement to ban chemical weapons.

I like to think that Helen and Mike and people like them played a part.

John Branfield, Cornwall, 1988

1
Leaving Home

The furniture van completely blocked the lane at the front gate of the house, and whenever any traffic came along the men had to stop loading and drive the van up the road to a wider stretch where the car could pass, and then back all the way down again. This was a nuisance, although luckily there was very little traffic using the road now the summer season was over. But the men had been delayed, and were getting bad-tempered.

If her father had been there, thought Helen, they would have tried to hide their impatience a bit more.

'Be careful!' she said, as one of them swung a picture off the wall and stacked it against another so that the corner of the frame was resting on the canvas of the painting beneath. It was one of her father's paintings, not one that he had done, but one that he had collected.

The man muttered under his breath, and moved the painting. He did not like being told off by a girl.

Her mother would not have said anything. She would not have complained if the canvas had been torn. She would have put up with it.

She was fussing around, quite helplessly. She was worrying about the cats and the dog and the children, but not doing anything about them. Anyway, everything had been done. The dog would go in the van at the last moment, and the cats were already in their basket, in case they roamed off when it was time to go.

'Helen, I wish I could make the men a cup of tea, I'm sure they expect it.'

The electricity supply had already been disconnected.

'Well, you can't,' said Helen.

'Perhaps I could boil a kettle on the range. There's still some fire in it.'

'Oh Mother!' said Helen. 'They don't even want any tea! All they're bothered about is finishing as soon as possible so that they don't lose their Saturday afternoon!'

'I think I ought to offer them something,' said Mrs Roberts.

And off she went to draw up the fire in the range, which Helen thought might boil a kettle by about midnight. At least, it gave her mother something to do.

The sitting room was almost bare now. The wallpaper must have faded, because where the paintings had hung there were darker shapes, like shadows. The fireplace seemed much more prominent. It was stone up to the beam below the ceiling, and she remembered when her father had taken out a tiled fireplace and the plaster above it. She remembered the large pieces with the perfect cast of the stone underneath. It had been many years ago.

The floorboards were varnished around the edge, and had unstained wood in the middle. Her footsteps echoed as she walked across them. Every room was the same, now that the house was practically empty. All were hollow and strange.

'Do you think we ought to have had them scrubbed?' asked her mother, coming to her. She seemed to think that Helen was staring at the dust in a corner. 'I suppose we should have done, but I really can't afford it, and I couldn't possibly do it myself.'

'How's the range?' asked Helen, a little sarcastically.

'Oh, it's coming up well,' said her mother. 'We might be able to have a cup of tea.'

'By tomorrow morning!' said Helen, but not bitterly. Her mother seemed unable to understand what was happening, and she suddenly felt sorry for her. She put her arm around her shoulder – she was two or three inches taller than her mother.

'What are the children doing?' asked Mrs Roberts.

'I'll go and see.'

Her footsteps clattered down the stairs. The house was cold

and empty. The front door was wide open, and the damp air was rushing in. There were muddy footmarks through the hall.

As she passed the kitchen door, their black and tan mongrel, Petra, leaped up from beside the range and came rushing out, thinking she was going for a walk.

'You'll be disappointed,' Helen warned her.

Outside on the front lawn were one or two pieces of furniture, still to go into the van – an old-fashioned wash-stand with a marble top, a chest of drawers, and the chair in which her father had always sat at the head of the table; she thought it was called a carver. They looked so incongruous out in the open. All her life – for she had always lived in this house – she had been used to seeing them in the same place, in the same room. And now they were exposed. It seemed so *wrong*. She felt she had to do something to put it right. But there was nothing that she could do. They were leaving, and she had to accept it.

She had always had a recurring dream in which they had to leave the house. It was a fear that had always been there, and now it was really happening. But in the last year even worse things had happened, things she had never even dreamt of, so that now when what had once seemed the worst came about, she could face it and know she would survive.

But it still seemed wrong. The furniture on the front lawn in the damp air was so disturbing. It was like the world turned upside-down, or inside-out.

She wondered about its effect on Paul. She looked around anxiously for her three-year-old brother.

He was sitting in the driver's cab of the pantechnicon, happily pulling on the wheel and making revving noises.

'I lorry driver,' he shouted.

Suddenly there was a screech of brakes as a car came around the bend. It stopped just short of the van, and Petra stood on the edge of the bank and barked furiously at it. Helen calmed the dog, and looked for Tom and Alison, her ten- and twelve-year-old brother and sister. They were supposed to be watching for traffic, and at the skid noise and barking they came running out of the field on the other side of the lane.

'Where were you two?' shouted Helen.

'There hadn't been any cars for hours,' said Alison.

'We went down in the field,' said Tom.

'It was your responsibility.'

'We got fed up.'

'Yes, it was too boring.'

'You could have caused a bad accident.'

'Stop being so bossy. You're always trying to boss us about. We didn't have to do it.'

The men had closed half the back of the van, and were driving up the road.

The car followed slowly behind.

'What were you doing in the field?' asked Helen.

'I went down to my house,' said Tom. 'Any objections?'

At the bottom end of the field was a thicket of elm saplings. They grew so close together no one could pass between them, and some years before Helen had started their interest in building by cutting a way through to the centre, and making a wattle hut. Using four growing trees as the corner posts, she had bound sticks between them with strips of bark peeled from the elms. As time went on she became more ambitious, enlarging the hut and making more use of the labour provided by the other two children. They had worked at it for hours, every holiday and sometimes at weekends when the building urge was on them. Helen had kept them at it. Whenever she took up an idea she would work at it as though some fury was possessing her. She would drive herself to exhaustion. She had had a passion for building and rebuilding the hut, and then she had dropped it completely and passed it on to Tom.

She thought of all the energy she had put into it. It could not be seen from outside, and could only be approached through the tightly spaced tree trunks by anyone who knew the path. It was a secret place. It was another part of herself that she was leaving behind with the house.

Tom and Alison ran up the road after the van. Helen turned back to the house, a grey stone and slate building fitting snugly against the hillside. A pale October sun just cleared the top of the hill, and cast a slanting light. The few windswept trees scrawled their shadows across the face of the house. She loved the place. When everything else in her world had been shattered, she wished at least that she could have held on to this. It was safe and secure, it was a refuge.

Tom and Alison did not mind leaving. In the village – it was more a small town really – Tom would be closer to his friends, and Alison only bothered about two things, a pony she borrowed and the youth club, and the new house would be much nearer and more convenient for both. Paul was too young to understand. It was Helen who felt it most.

She whistled to the dog, and walked up to the top of the garden. She went right to the highest corner, where her father had always had his bonfires, but where she had always thought that one day she would have a hut, a proper wooden one, a summerhouse where she could paint and write and stay away from the family for days at a time. And now in future she would not even have a bedroom of her own.

From its window she would have looked across the sloping lawn and over the tops of the trees and beyond the roofs of the outbuildings and the back of the house and down the steep sides of the valley to the V at the end, filled in with the sea. The four pots on the massive end-chimney were in the bottom of the V, a brownish pink against the slate colour of the sea. The sides of the hills were pale at this time of the year with the summer's dried grass, which had grown taller than the heather, and then withered; lower down it was brown with dead bracken.

The only building in the valley was the old engine house of a mine, now in ruins, but the chimney stood tall against the side of the hill.

She tried to absorb the whole scene, to capture it so that it would be hers for ever. Once she had left she would never return. She would have to pass along the road in the school bus every morning, but she ought to be able to avoid ever walking by, as it was only a small lane and there was an alternative route. From the village she would come back to the valley and cliffs and moors. But she would never return to this house and this garden.

This is how I shall always remember it, she told herself. With the slight mist and the sea merging into the sky, the place had a look of mystery about it. A white cat stalked along the bottom of a stone bank. A few seagulls flew untidily from one side of the valley to the other, and cried wildly. The tree-tops swayed, all bending away from the coast, their growth checked by the sea-winds. The bare branches were wet and shining. The damp slates of the house glistened.

She had to take in every detail. She had to miss nothing. This was the last time.

But she was trying too hard, and it did not work. It did not seem quite so significant as she had expected it to be, and she laughed at herself for being too intense.

'Come on, Petra,' she called. 'Have your last sniff at the ashes. You won't smell those again.'

Then she ran down the slope, slithering on the wet grass and only keeping her balance on the steepest bank beneath the ash tree by grabbing hold of the rope that hung from the lowest bough. It remained from a swing they had once played on – her father had fixed it up for her as soon as she had been old enough, although at first it had frightened her because you started well up on the slope with your feet on the ground, but as you swung forward the ground fell away and you were high in the air, flying it seemed away over the valley. She could remember screaming, the first time she had been launched into flight. And her father stopping the swing and comforting her.

Now one grey rope, with a knot in the end, hung out of the tree; it had been left to help people steady themselves on the embankment. It checked Helen's headlong rush and changed her course as she swung through part of a circle and ran on down the rest of the slope at more of an angle.

Petra was running too, getting under her feet. She thought it was a game and expected Helen to chase her back up the lawn, where she would allow herself to be nearly caught, but always escape at the last moment. But this time Helen did not stop. Without looking back, she ran on through the garden, down the steps to the back yard and into the house. She arrived breathless in the kitchen.

'Helen!' exclaimed her mother in triumph. 'I've got the kettle to boil!'

It was true, it was just beginning to steam on the range.

'You thought I wouldn't be able to do it,' went on Mrs Roberts. 'But I knew I could. Now you just get the things and I'll make the men a cup of tea.'

Helen went out to the scullery. There were empty shelves, bare walls, a sink and a draining board. Even the tea chests into which the crockery and utensils had been packed were gone.

She returned to the kitchen.

'Mother,' she said, beginning to put on a long-suffering tone of voice.

Her mother turned around from the range, hot-faced and smiling. Then she saw that Helen was empty-handed, and her face fell.

'It's all been packed,' said Helen, gently.

And then she giggled, and as her mother looked up she said, 'Oh, I'm sorry,' but giggled more, tried to restrain herself and started to laugh.

Her mother looked for a moment as though she might cry, and then she too laughed. They laughed together.

'No tea, no tea-pot, no cups, no saucers!' said Mrs Roberts, laughing more and more helplessly at each item.

'Only a kettle of boiling water!'

The noise of their laughter was uncanny in the now completely empty house.

'The men will be here in a minute,' said her mother. 'We must take control of ourselves.'

She burst out laughing again.

'Oh dear, they'll think we're quite mad.'

Helen emptied the kettle, and they locked up. It seemed a shame that the next owners had bought the house as a holiday residence. They would never know the house in all seasons and weathers; for much of the year it would stand empty and uncared for.

They walked out to the van, Helen swinging the kettle in one hand. The foreman was reluctant to take them as passengers; he said it was a matter of insurance.

'But it's only two or three miles,' pleaded Mrs Roberts.

He supposed he could risk it this once. They all climbed into the back of the van with the furniture, and Petra jumped in. Their possessions took up very little space. The doors slammed, and they were imprisoned in the gloomy interior, all the Roberts, and all they had, shut up in one big box.

Mrs Roberts began worrying again, about how large a tip the men would expect, and Helen was opposed to giving any tip at all.

'We would have had to hire a taxi,' her mother pointed out. They had sold the car after her father died.

Suddenly the van jolted forwards and they were all thrown off their balance to the back of the van. Most of the furniture shifted and held, but an unsecured settee came hurtling down the van on its castors, knocking Tom off his feet and pinning Alison and her mother against the door.

'We must all push', cried Mrs Roberts. 'Wedge it against the door.'

They all pushed hard, but when the van stopped at the bottom of the hill, the settee was off again and they could not hold it. It scooped up the pushers in its path and raced down to the furniture in the forward end of the van.

'It's not good enough! They ought to have fastened it, it'll be knocked to pieces. My best settee!'

The family gave up trying to hold it and all sat on, keeping their feet up. At bends in the road it rushed from side to side and on gradients, or stopping and starting, it zoomed up and

8

down. It was like a dodgem car at a fairground.

The younger chidren laughed because it was funny and exciting. And Helen and her mother laughed, as they glided and bumped on their way from the old home, because if they had not laughed they would have cried.

2
Doubts

The doors of the van were flung open and the light flooded into the interior. The tailboard was dropped and the Roberts family, looking rather dazzled in the brightness and a little unsteady on their feet after the shaking-up of the journey, stepped down into the street.

Like travellers arriving out of space, thought Helen. She helped Paul to jump, and Petra followed.

Already a crowd of children from the estate had gathered behind the van, and Tom seeing some of his friends went and joined them, with a slight air of importance because this was his family moving in.

Helen had seen the house before, but she had not yet been inside. All the houses on the estate were the same, pairs of semi-detached houses placed close together. She thought they were called Cornish unit houses – there were a lot of them in the county. They were made of cement sections, and the upstairs wall was not a wall but a continuation of the roof, sloping very steeply and jutting out slightly beyond the ground floor. They never looked right to Helen; they looked like people with hats pulled down over their eyes and ears.

There was a wooden gate in a block wall, a small patch of long grass, and then they were at the front door. Mrs Roberts had the key, a small Yale key unlike the big iron keys at home, and as soon as the door was opened, the younger children, accompanied by several of the children from the street, rushed in. They ran all over the house. It did not take long.

'Isn't it small!' said Alison.

Helen agreed. Upstairs there were two bedrooms, a box

room just big enough to take a single bed and nothing else, and a bathroom; downstairs the hall, kitchen and living room.

But it was the shape of the rooms which struck her most. She was used to low beams downstairs, and sloping ceilings in the bedrooms. Here the rooms were as high as they were long, and very square. They seemed to her like boxes.

There were thirteen steps on the stairs, instead of eleven.

'I'm having the back bedroom,' said Alison. 'I've laid claim to it. It's mine now.'

'Bags I have the little room,' said Tom.

They had all gathered on the landing.

'Where my room, Mummy?' asked Paul.

'You won't be able to have a room each, I'm afraid,' said Mrs Roberts. 'You'll have to share.'

'I'm not sharing with Helen,' said Alison.

'I think that would be best. If you and Helen have the back bedroom . . .'

'Oh no!' said Tom. 'I don't want to share with Paul. He's a nuisance!'

'I'd rather share with Tom,' said Alison. 'And then Helen can have Paul. She usually looks after him anyway.'

'No, I think the girls ought to be together, and the boys together, especially as you're getting older. It will have to be that way later on, so you might as well start now. What do you think, Helen?'

'I suppose so.'

For once her mother seemed to be having her own way. 'And I'll have the small room in the front,' Mrs Roberts added.

'I'm not sharing with *her*,' said Alison in a voice full of disgust as she looked at Helen.

'Well, you'll have to.'

'I don't see why we had to move anyway. We could have stayed at home and kept our own rooms.'

'Alison, you know very well,' said Mrs Roberts. 'We had no alternative.'

Helen was inclined to agree with Alison, though she would

not have chosen this moment to say so. They had argued about little else in the past three months. She had thought they could manage to stay on in the house, although she admitted there were many difficulties. But now that they had moved, there was no point in going over the old arguments again. It was done, and could not be changed.

'You could have made it a guest house. We wouldn't have minded sharing just for the summer. Or we could have camped in the field.'

'We could have slept in our hut,' added Tom.

'Alison, you just don't understand. There was a mortgage on the house.'

'Well, we've got to pay rent now.'

'Mum has only got a small pension,' put in Helen. 'It's not very much, you know.'

'We could have made a lot of money taking visitors.'

'That's only for a short while. It's very uncertain. And then there were other things. But I'm not going over all that again, it's finished with now. The old house was too much for me. It's going to be easier here – if you'll all co-operate.'

'I don't mind living here,' said Tom. 'I like it.'

'Helen doesn't like it,' said Alison, 'because she's a snob. She doesn't like it because it's a council house.'

'That's not true!' snapped Helen. 'It was you who started it. You said you didn't want to come here. I didn't say anything.'

'I didn't want to come here because I don't want to share with you. I don't mind the place.'

'Please, children,' begged their mother. 'Don't start that now! We're lucky to have a house at all.'

Helen went off into the back bedroom. She looked out of the window. There were the backs of another row of houses like theirs, and beyond that the even line of the roofs of terrace houses, the miners' cottages that lined the main street of the village, with a few trees rising above them, and the end gable of a chapel and a spire and a few chimneys of engine houses.

She did not like the semi-detached houses, but it was not

because they were council houses. She disliked the new and expensive bungalows along the coast road even more. It was not snobbish to want people to live in houses that looked good, as the old houses did because they were made out of the slate and stone of the district and belonged to the landscape. Some new houses could do it, it was not just a matter of money. But the accusation hurt her, and she thought that perhaps there was some truth in it.

'I am a bit snobbish,' she admitted.

She could understand, though, why her mother had sold the old house. It had been expensive to run. A car was essential, as it was too far to walk into the village, and now they could manage without. It really was too large for her mother to manage on her own. When their father was alive he had always been mending and repairing. An old house needed a lot of looking after, and it would have cost a lot to pay a builder to do the odd jobs that her father had always done.

They would have had to make enough money out of the house to cover its upkeep. Helen would not have hesitated to stay on. In her mother's place she would have taken the risk of making a success of it.

But her mother wanted no more risks, she had chosen security. With the mortgage paid off and the balance from the sale of the house invested, she had just enough, when it was added to her pension, to live on. Or at least, to exist on. For it would only enable a very quiet, cautious way of life. Her mother had no qualifications for any particular job, and Paul was not yet at school. She had settled for the little that was safe, and Helen could understand why she needed to do this. But it would not have been her way.

Standing at the window, she noticed how thin the ledge was; the wall had no thickness in it at all. She realised how cold it was in the room. At home all the windows had deep window seats, the walls were three or four feet thick.

No, she told herself. She must stop it, she must make no more comparisons. This was where she lived now. This was home.

13

Already the men had laid the floor coverings, and were now bringing in the heavier pieces of furniture. Helen set to and did what she could to help. The younger children were diving into the van to bring out their own possessions. Paul had dragged out his tricycle and pedal car, and kept leaving them on the path in the way of men carrying wardrobes and beds. She tried to persuade him to play at the back, but this was not nearly so interesting, so she let him sit in his car on the pavement, and kept an eye on him to see that he did not go in the road. Tom had soon recovered his bicycle, guitar and fishing rod. Alison fetched the two cats in their box.

The removal men had their own ideas about where the furniture ought to go.

'If there isn't a man in the house,' Mrs Roberts complained, 'they think they can get away with anything!'

So Helen told them where the pieces were to go, when she could get her mother to decide. Otherwise, she made the decisions herself. In a different setting, the furniture seemed familiar and yet strange. They had sold quite a lot by advertising it in the local paper, but they still had too much for the house, and the rooms began to look overcrowded.

'We can sort it out afterwards,' she told her mother, who was getting very flustered again.

The men seemed concerned only to get everything out of the van and into the house. It was coming faster than Mrs Roberts could cope with it.

In a short time everything was unloaded, the foreman had received a tip which Helen thought was far too much, and the van was off down the street followed by a group of boys, including Tom, on bikes.

'I don't know how we'll ever get straight!' said Mrs Roberts with a sigh. 'I don't know where to begin. And look at the time!'

It was half past one.

'Let's have something to eat, and then we can make the place tidy afterwards.'

'I don't know what we'll have, I haven't got anything in.'

'Send Tom for some fish and chips.'

Helen went out to call him in off the street, and saw that Paul was in the road. She blamed Tom, who denied that it was his responsibility, and she was cross with Paul, who howled and ran to his mother. Tom and Alison went off with some money. By the time they were back, a pot of tea had been brewed, and the whole family sat around the table in the living room, with cups of tea and the fish and chips still wrapped in newspaper. Paul sat on his mother's lap sucking chips; the others tucked in hungrily. The room smelt of frying fat.

'This is all right,' said Tom. 'I like being able to go out and buy fish and chips. We can do it every day.'

They ate with their fingers, dipping into the greasy paper. Helen glanced at her mother, and wondered if she was thinking of their father. To her it seemed impossible not to think of him at this moment, because it was so much what he would have hated. He liked things to be orderly – perhaps it was to do with being a scientist. He could not have stood a meal like this.

But clearly her mother was not thinking of him. For Paul had a hot chip that was burning his mouth, and he was yelling and she was using her little finger to hook out the half-chewed pieces of potato, and shouting, 'For heaven's sake, get a glass of water! Don't just sit there, won't anybody move?'

Helen stood up, and fetched the water.

As she worked that afternoon, helping her mother to put some order into the house, she thought of another reason why her mother might be glad to leave the old home. For there, everything was a reminder of her father. She had found herself thinking of him all the time, there was something of him in every room. It was not only his possessions, like paintings and books; nor the signs of his work, like the stone fireplace and the pine dresser he had stripped to the natural wood. There were all these reminders of him and more: he had slept in this room until he finally went to hospital a week before his death, he had

15

worked at the bench in the old stables, he had planted shrubs – wild ones, mostly, broom and heather – in the garden. The house was so much an expression of himself, that when he had gone his presence was still there. It was almost as though it was haunted.

And although the new house still contained the furniture he had used, and his paintings and books, and she still could not help thinking of him from time to time, Helen realised that it was going to be different. There was no feeling of his still being there.

She supposed that this was what her mother wanted. It would have been very difficult for her to accept his loss, when all the time she felt that he was still close.

And yet, Helen regretted this. She did not want to accept his loss, she still wanted to be reminded of him. Perhaps she loved her father more than her mother had. Or perhaps, when you grow older, you feel less keenly and get over things more quickly. She did not want to forget.

Especially when there were some things about her father's death that she did not understand. It was still a mystery to her, how a man who was so strong and healthy could within a year fall ill and die. If he had always been ill she could have understood it. Or if he had been killed in an accident, it would have been more sudden and more of a shock, but there would have been a reason for it. He had always been so active. He played rugby and tennis, he liked walking and sailing. He had always been doing something. And then suddenly he had become very tired. He had fought against it, like a man trying to keep awake. He had struggled desperately, but it had overcome him like a great drowsiness. He had simply gone to sleep in the middle of his life.

Why? Helen wanted to know. Why had it happened to him? Was it something he had caught, or had it always been lurking within him? She had never had any satisfactory answers to her questions. Whenever she tried to speak about it, her mother always avoided the subject. She knew that it was painful to her, but she wanted to know.

She found it difficult to find an opportunity to talk about it, when her mother so obviously did not want to be reminded. She had suffered, and was now trying to forget. But Helen was still suffering, and would continue to suffer until she knew the truth.

Why had her father died? She knew that everyone who had lost a relation would feel like this, but she was certain, too, that there were some strange aspects of her father's death that had never been explained.

He had worked at Nancekuke. It was the outpost of Porton Down, part of the Ministry of Defence. At Nancekuke they made gas for riot control, and her father had done research on chemical weapons.

He had been strong and healthy, and suddenly he had sickened and died. He had been working on poisonous gases.

The authorities said there was no connection, but Helen thought it was very suspicious.

3
A Last Request

They worked hard all the afternoon, arranging the furniture, making the beds, packing things away. Helen found time to slip out and do some shopping for the weekend. She was determined that their tea that evening should be special, a sort of celebration for the start of their new life, even if she herself felt more like mourning the past than celebrating the future. It became very important to her, and she spent some of her own money on buying a block of ice-cream, fancy cakes, splits and chocolate biscuits. She wished she had had time to do some baking herself, and make trifles and jellies.

She set the table very carefully, so that it looked as though it was all ready for a party. She washed Paul, and made Tom do his hair. Alison returned from riding; she knew better than to try and get her to change. She had some influence on the boys, but not on Alison.

'It looks lovely, dear!' said Mrs Roberts.

They all sat down.

'It's my birthday,' said Paul. He sang 'Happy Birthday' in a high, shouting voice. 'It's my birthday in June.' He began singing again.

'I know, let's have a competition,' said his mother brightly. 'Let's see who can keep quiet the longest.'

There was two seconds' silence.

'I not playing this game,' said Paul, and got down from his chair.

'Sit up!' said Helen.

He went whining to his mother. 'I want to go to the bathroom.'

'Isn't it wonderful!' said Mrs Roberts. 'The moment I sit down, it's always the same. Someone else take him.'

'I will,' said Helen.

'I want my mummy to take me.'

'Oh, come on then. Hurry up!'

They left the room.

Tom ate with great concentration, crouching over his food as though he expected it to be snatched from him at any moment.

'Sit up straight,' said Helen.

He did not look at her, but slouched lower over his plate, pushing his arms further out along the table.

'Stop being so bossy!' said Alison.

'Bossy boots!' echoed Tom.

Helen leaned forward and pushed his elbow off the table. He struck out at her arm. Mrs Roberts returned with Paul.

'I've just thought of a joke,' said Tom. 'What happens to a man who falls into a sewer?'

'Oh, not at the tea-table!'

'I don't know.'

'He commits sewer-cide!'

Groans from both girls, and cries of 'sick' and 'pathetic'. Tom just carried on eating.

'I know a joke,' shouted Paul. 'Knock, knock! Who's there? Nobody.' He shrieked with laughter. 'That's a rude joke,' he added seriously.

'Why's he got such a loud voice?'

'It's the only way he can make himself heard against you all.'

'Anyway, Tom, I bet you didn't make that joke up,' said Alison.

'I did.'

'I bet you read it in a book.'

'I didn't. I made it up myself.'

'Bloody liar!'

'Alison, there's no need to swear,' said Mrs Roberts. 'You can call him a liar, without —'

'She can't call me a liar. I did think of it myself.'

'It doesn't matter, does it, whether it was made up or not.'

'She's a liar!'

'It's so unimportant.'

'Did you see that letter in your magazine?' asked Helen.

'You shouldn't be reading my magazine.'

'It was from a girl who wanted to give up swearing.'

'Shut up!'

'You'll have to put sixpence in the swear box, Alison.'

There was no such box. Mrs Roberts was always saying she would impose fines for swearing, but she had never done anything about it.

'Why is it always horsey girls who swear?'

'Shut up!'

Paul began echoing his sister, shouting 'Shut up! Shut up!' He had taken a cake, eaten off the icing and threw the rest of the cake on the floor.

'Hell, Mother,' said Alison. 'Why don't you make him behave? If I had children I'd make them do what I wanted. I'd knock them about if they didn't. You're too soft with him, woman.'

Their mother said nothing, not even complaining at the way she spoke to her.

Alison turned on Paul. 'Pick it up!' she bellowed, as though she was dealing with a difficult pony.

Paul started crying and ran to his mother. She comforted him.

'He misses his father,' she quietly. 'We all do.'

There was a hush, broken only by Paul's sobbing. Mrs Roberts gave him his dummy, and he was still.

Helen wanted to go on talking about their father, now that her mother had for once referred to him. But she did not know how to, not with the other children there.

'I'm sorry, dear,' Mrs Roberts said to Helen. 'You took so much trouble, I hope we haven't spoilt it for you.'

Alison got up, as though she thought the last remark was

aimed at her in some way. 'I'm going to have a bath, she said. 'I'm going to the youth club dance.'

'It doesn't matter,' said Helen. 'About the tea.'

She wondered if every family was like this. Everyone at school said that all families quarrelled. But she was sure that it had not been like this when their father was alive. There was an edginess about them when they were all together. They were all changing. Her mother had never been quite so helpless, and Alison was becoming much harder. Tom had grown more quiet, coming out only with his sick jokes. Paul was badly behaved, and easily upset.

What effect was it having on her? She was trying to force them all to stay as they had been, to keep everything the same. That was attempting the impossible, a sort of King Canute act. She had to see that it could not stay the same.

Paul unstoppered the dummy from his mouth. 'I don't like this house,' he said. 'I want to go home.'

When the tea-things were cleared, Helen went up to the bedroom. Alison had her clothes all over the floor and both beds. If they were going to share, Helen could see that she would be spending a lot of time moving her sister's belongings into her half of the room. She had no intention of packing them away.

Alison came barging in. 'What a house!' she complained. 'There isn't any ruddy hot water.'

'There's an immersion, but it hasn't been on long.'

'I had a freezing bath.'

'Here, take your clothes,' said Helen, beginning to pick up the jumpers and jeans on the bed by the window.

'No, that's my bed,' said Alison. 'I've claimed it.'

'Looks to me as if you've claimed them both.'

She cleared the bed by the door, and they agreed on wall space for their pictures and cuttings. The room was going to look very odd, with Alison's half all ponies and pop groups, and Helen's half covered with posters. They also divided the dressing table down the middle.

Alison was getting dressed for the dance. Helen had to admit, rather grudgingly, that she looked very striking. She had magnificent auburn hair, which she wore very long. She was tall and well-built, and looked much older than twelve. She put on cords and a skinnyrib jumper.

'You aren't going to wear that, are you?' asked Helen.

'You sound just like Mother.'

'But you can see through it.'

'That's the fashion.'

'You can see your nipples.'

Alison examined herself in the mirror. 'Will you lend me a bra, Helen?'

'It wouldn't fit you.'

But she found an old one and Alison stuffed the cups with pink tissues from the box on the dressing table.

When she put the skinnyrib on again the pink glowed through from underneath. The two girls collapsed on their beds with laughter.

Alison started again, this time wearing pinky white tights, a flowery pink blouse and a brown cord pinafore dress. The pink ought to have looked wrong with her chestnut hair, but somehow she carried it off. That was how it always was with Alison, she never gave any thought to her clothes, but whatever she put on she looked beautiful. Helen could easily feel jealous of her. She felt that whatever she wore immediately became dull and ordinary, however well-chosen it had been in the first place. Alison never bothered.

Physically she took after her father, while Helen resembled her mother. On their side of the family they were slim to the point of thinness, with dark eyes and black hair. Although she was taller than Alison, there did not seem to be much difference in their heights, as Helen stood in a rather drooping sort of way. Tom had the same stance, which was why it annoyed her in him. Paul, with his ginger hair and freckles, was going to be like his father.

Getting dressed up for the dance made Alison excited, and

the two girls had become quite sisterly. It did not seem for the moment as though it would be too bad having to share.

'Do my eyes for me, 'len.'

'All right, Liz.'

Alison sat on the edge of the bed, underneath the central, single light in the room, and held her face up to Helen, whilst she applied the liner.

'Close your eyes, Liz.'

She put a black line along the lids.

'Open them and look up.'

Another line beneath the lower lashes.

'There, how's that?'

Alison flashed her eyes in the mirror of the dressing table, looking at herself first over one shoulder and then over the other, giving a twist inwards with her shoulder and spreading the palm of her hand out.

'It's not enough,' she said.

'You don't want too much.'

Alison took the brush and added a touch of her own.

'That'll do,' she said, with satisfaction.

Helen thought she had ruined the effect.

'Why don't you come?' Alison asked.

'I don't feel like it.'

'It'll be great, man,' said Alison. She stood on her toes, tucked her elbows in to her sides, and jiggled her arms up and down.

'You gotta get out, man. It don't do no good to stay in brooding. You gotta start livin', man.'

Each time she said 'man' she gave it a long, drawled, American vowel. And all the time she jigged about, swinging her legs from side to side.

'I know, you're right.'

Her mother was always telling her the same thing, in a different way. 'You haven't got enough interests, Helen. I wish you'd be more like Alison. I wish you'd go riding and to the youth club. I wish you'd make more friends. You're rather a lonely girl.'

Helen would cringe.

'Then why don't you come?' asked Alison again. She posed and coquetted in front of the mirror. 'Pete'll be there.'

'I'm not interested.'

'He asked if you were going.'

She had been out with Peter once or twice. She was not very keen on him. They had been to a dance, and the music was so loud that you could only shout to each other, and then you could not hear much. It was all rather boring. She had seen her sister at the last youth club discotheque she had been to. Alison would dance with a boy and then sit kissing with him in the back seats, and ten minutes later she would be there with another boy.

'No, I'm going to stay at home and do my half of the room.'

'You can put up my pictures if you like. Shall I give Pete a message?'

'No, thanks.'

'I'll just give him your love then.'

'No!'

'All right! All right! Don't get so touchy!'

'You needn't say anything.' Alison was at the age when they were continually arranging friendships for one another. 'My boyfriend's got a friend who hasn't got a girlfriend, so if you come with me . . .' Helen did not want to be fixed up with anyone, especially by Alison.

'Well, bye then!' said Alison with a wave. 'Be good, and don't do anything I wouldn't do.'

She went out. That was one thing I couldn't do, thought Helen. I couldn't make that last remark.

'Snob,' she called herself. She felt very lonely, as her mother said.

She just sat on the bed for a while, until the coldness of the room made her move. She wondered if they would be able to have a point put in for an electric fire and a bedside lamp. How did you arrange it when it was not your own house?

The walls had a picture rail around them; it was quite useful for pinning things to. She put up her Habitat calendar, its enormous black numbers still showing the month of June.

She had some big tissue paper flowers she had made herself, and she pinned these through the centre. Some posters she sellotaped to the wall, a fashion drawing of a girl smothered in flowers, all reds, pinks and purples, and, inexplicably, a map of Ceylon. Her largest poster was of Steve McQueen, almost life-size, from 'I Was Lord Kitchener's Valet'. He stood behind a desk against a highly patterned wallpaper, in white Levis and a blue, open-necked shirt.

He looked very much like her father. Just a bit more glamorous, perhaps.

Over the head of the bed she fixed a German poster. It was announcing a performance: MOZART OPER BRUNNEN-HOF was in large print across the bottom with details of times and prices. Above this was a seventeenth-century print of a palace courtyard, with a statue in the middle and men on horseback and walking, with swords sticking out from under their coat-tails. The whole poster was in blues and white, with lots of scrolls and curls.

Her father had brought it home from Germany. He had been to the open-air opera. There was some mystery about why he went to Germany. He had gone on his own, and it had not been a holiday. It was to do with his work, some sort of business trip. He had never said very much about it, he never talked about his work.

But Helen wondered about this visit, because it was not long afterwards that he began to be ill, having spells of dizziness and faintness. Could there be any connection between his going to Germany and his becoming a sick man? If so, what was it? And how could she ever hope to find out? It all seemed impossibly difficult. How could she solve it, when everyone else saw nothing particularly strange in his death? For them it was sad that a man should be cut off in the middle of life, particularly when he had a wife and family. But there was nothing unnatural nor suspect about it. Only Helen had this burden to carry, the belief that his death could have been avoided. It was her responsibility to find out the truth, and she had one possible line of inquiry.

She turned to a cardboard box of books and records, and started unpacking them. There was one small bookcase in the room and they had agreed to have two shelves each. Helen arranged her books glancing occasionally at the titles or opening them and banging them shut when they looked particularly dusty, until she came to the book she was looking for.

It was a brown, leather-covered (probably plastic) address book, with padded covers, golden edges to the pages at the top, and the alphabet cut out in steps down the side. It had been given to her as a birthday present when she was seven or eight.

She flicked through the pages. There were the addresses, in childish handwriting, of all their friends and neighbours, her French pen-friend, an Italian boy who had stopped writing to her, some addresses her mother had wanted her to include, like those of the piano tuner and the dentist, the vet for Petra and the cats, and then the address she was looking for, almost the last entry in the book: William Wyatt.

In his last week at home before going into hospital, her father one day had come into her bedroom in his dressing-gown and sat down on the bed, as he quite often did. They had talked for a while, and there were times when he seemed to doze. Then he said very casually, 'By the way, do you still have that old address book of yours?'

'Yes.'

'Let's have a look at it.'

'If you want to.' She passed it from the shelf.

He looked it through. 'Who on earth is Margaret Randles?' he asked. 'Of Birmingham.'

'She was here on holiday.'

'I don't remember her.'

He was silent for a while. Then he said. 'It's funny, an address book, isn't it? It makes you feel the difference of other people's lives.'

'Mine must be very empty then!'

'It'll fill up.'

Another pause.

'I've got Bill Wyatt's address,' he said suddenly.

'I don't know him.'

'Will you write it down?'

'But I don't know him.' She thought her father, taking pity on her, just wanted to fill her book. He was treating her as though she was a small child again. 'I don't want his address.'

'Please, Helen,' he said, in a tone so different that she looked up, startled. 'Just write it down for me.'

So she wrote down the address in London that he dictated, in order to humour him, wondering too why it seemed to matter. 'Who is he?' she asked.

'Just a friend.'

He seemed very tired, and closed his eyes. Helen thought he was sleeping again, but after a while he murmured, 'I'd like you to have it. You never know, it might be useful.'

Helen at the time could not see how it could ever be of any use, when she did not even know the man. For she had known that her father was very ill, but she had not known that he was dying. He must have realised that the end was near, and given her the address for a purpose.

He must have wanted her to tell his old friend of his death. Helen found it very moving, that her father could calmly make this arrangement.

She had not written before, because she thought it could not be a matter of urgency, and she did not want to seem to be asking Mr Wyatt for help in any way. She had waited until they were in the new house. There was now nothing he could do for them, and he need not feel under any obligation.

Her writing materials were in the same box, and she wrote with the pad on her knee. The room was not very convenient for writing in, but at least Alison was out a lot of the time. It would have been dreadful if they had both wanted to spend much time indoors. A table and lamp were essentials.

She wrote the new address very deliberately, conscious that she was using it for the first time. Then she went on:

Dear Mr Wyatt,

Please forgive me for writing to you if you already know what I have to tell you, or if the news is of no concern to you. My father, Thomas Maxwell Roberts, died on June 27th last, and just before his death he gave me your address. As he knew he was dying, I can only presume it was to enable me to write this letter.

We have moved to this address and are managing very well. Please do not feel any need to reply, but should you need any further information I should be pleased to supply it.

Yours faithfully,

Helen Roberts

She read it through, and despaired. What a cold, priggish letter it sounded! Why did she have to make it sound like a solicitor writing, as though she had no feelings at all? She wished she was more spontaneous.

She tried out a few alternatives, but settled for the first draft. After all, it said all that was needed. And she might never hear anything more of Mr Wyatt. She had been hoping that he might possibly know something about her father that she did not know, but it was most unlikely when he apparently knew nothing of his illness and had had no contact with him in recent years. She could not expect to find out anything new from him.

The letter was now ready for posting, and she decided to send it off that night, even though there was no collection until the next day. She told her mother, who was watching television, that she was slipping out to give Petra her nightly walk, and then, with the dog on an unaccustomed lead, they went through the estate and into the village.

There were coloured light bulbs around the front of the cinema (which was an old converted chapel), a splash of light from a café, and pop music blared out from the hall where the youth club dance was taking place.

Life in the big city, she muttered to herself.

She went on to the post office, and dropped the letter into the box.

4
The Gas Factory

The school bus left the village at a quarter to eight, and then meandered through the countryside collecting children from cottages, hamlets and villages to get them to school by nine o'clock. It had passed their old house just before eight, stopping to pick them up. But on Monday morning they had to be up and into the village a good quarter of an hour earlier than usual. A quarter of an hour did not seem very much, but at that time of the morning it made all the difference. It had always been a hectic rush to be ready, and Helen had usually been at the gate screaming 'Alison, it's coming!' as the bus eased its way down the narrow lane from the top of the hill, and Alison would come dashing out of the house, still eating toast and marmalade, her bulging satchel spilling books along the path.

But now there was no keeping a look-out for it, and they knew it would not wait. To make things worse, their mother's alarm had not gone off. Suddenly she had put her head around the door and woken them with a shriek: 'It's twenty-five to eight!'

They had tumbled out of bed and into their clothes, Alison swearing because she could not find the clean underwear she wanted. Their mother, in her nightie, rushed around, pulling out drawers, but nothing was yet in the expected places.

'You should have put it ready last night,' she grumbled. 'I told you to.'

'Christ, Mother! You're not organised.'

'You're old enough to organise yourself.'

Eventually some suitable garments were assembled, and they hurried downstairs, Alison clomping on the treads.

'Hush! You'll wake Tom and Paul. They're still sleeping.'
Tom was in his last year at the village primary school.

'I don't care.'

'Alison!'

In the kitchen Mrs Roberts tried to prepared some breakfast.

'We can't stop,' said Helen.

'But you must have something. You can't go off to school on empty stomachs.'

Helen tried to swallow cornflakes fast; they scratched her throat. Alison sat down very deliberately, slowly covered her cornflakes with sugar and took the cream from a new bottle of milk.

'You haven't time,' said Mrs Roberts. 'You're going to miss the bus.'

'I don't care.'

'You're trying to have the day off. You're going to school today, I insist.'

Alison ate on, chewing every mouthful several times.

'Where's your satchel?'

'I don't know.'

'Really, Alison. You don't help at all. You ought to look after your things.'

The door crashed open, and Paul stood there, wearing only pyjama tops. 'I want a drinkie,' he announced.

'You'll have to wait a minute, Paul,' said Mrs Roberts, rushing around looking for the satchel.

'I want a drinkie,' shouted Paul.

'Why did you wake him up? I've got to get the girls off first. It's gone twenty to.'

Paul began to howl. Mrs Roberts found the satchel. She took hold of Alison by the arm and collar, and dragged her from the table. She hooked her satchel over her shoulder, and propelled her towards the door. Helen opened it, Alison was pushed through, and the door slammed.

Helen could still hear Paul crying as she half-walked, half-ran down the street, followed some distance behind by Alison.

But they were in time for the bus, and when Alison came up she joined her friends and started chatting gaily to them, as though she had been up for hours and had had a charming, leisurely breakfast.

A moment later the bus drew up, and Alison and her friends pushed and scrambled to be first aboard, so that they could grab the back seats.

'Hey, I haven't had any breakfast,' Alison shouted to a boy. 'Lend me a fag!'

The smoked and laughed and made a lot of noise for the rest of the journey.

Helen sat further forward, apart from the others, and looked out of the window. The bus left the village, and climbed up one side of the headland behind which the village sheltered. From this bare, windswept slope, she could see all along the North Cliffs as far as Godrevy Island with its lighthouse, at the opening of St Ives Bay. The land swept in treeless, faded-brown moors to the edge of the cliffs; at their feet the sea broke in white foam. She could see the waves crashing against the rocks, rising up and flowering for a moment before falling back.

The whole landscape was pale and rain-washed. Some miles away a chimney stood like a stroke against the sky, the only vertical in the horizontal stretch of the downs and valleys. It broke an otherwise smooth skyline. There were a few buildings clustered around it, lost in the empty miles of moorland.

This was Nancekuke. It always seemed incredible to Helen, whenever she saw the tall chimney, that on this wild and beautiful coast men could even consider making poison gas. It made her shudder.

And yet her father had been one of these men. He never told them anything about his job; whenever they asked him he said it was a secret, and he had sworn not to tell. 'The Official Secrets Act,' he would say with a smile.

It was only quite recently that they had learnt what was made at Nancekuke – and then they discovered it from the papers and television, not from their father. A member of parliament had asked questions in the House of Commons, and the answers revealed that it was to do with gas warfare. For a few days it made news, and was in all the papers and on news programmes. It seemed strange hearing the name they were so familiar with, on the national news. And quite often the announcers could not say it correctly, making it sound like a girl's name, or an African tribe. It was Nance, in one syllable; kuke, to rhyme with duke, Nancekuke.

It was a surprise to find out what went on there, because their father had never breathed the slightest hint that it had anything to do with gas, not even to their mother. It was a shock too. When they were smaller they had always been able to gain a certain standing by saying, 'My father works at Nancekuke. It's secret.'

There had been a lot of rumours about the place. All sorts of stories went around the primary school. They said there were cages with rabbits in all around the high fence, and if ever the rabbits died, then everyone in Cornwall would die too. They said that the men there worked in asbestos suits, and they looked like spacemen. They said it was guarded by furious Alsatians that ran along inside the wire. But when the children asked their father he would only smile and answer non-committally, 'Maybe . . . sometimes.' They could never get anything exciting out of him, and they felt cheated because they ought to be in a position to know more than the others. And the subject was an exciting one, to all the children in the primary school. The Roberts were not the only children with a father working at Nancekuke, but whether they had relatives there or not, it haunted their imaginations. They dreamt about it, and brought it into their paintings. It was a mystery, the big, secret place of the real world.

She had been questioned sometimes by curious grown-ups, who thought she might have heard her father talking. She had always felt very responsible, and given nothing away, even though she had nothing she could give away. They had suggested that it was an emergency seat of government (there was

33

a landing strip which might have given that impression). Others thought that it was to do with atomic research. Another popular theory was that radio-active waste was brought there, taken down a mine shaft, and stored in tunnels stretching out far under the sea.

So she had grown up believing her father's work was very important and secret; it was special. And then it turned out that it was just a dirty gas factory.

But her father had already left, not being well enough to continue work. And to her it seemed so obvious that she could not understand why it was not equally obvious to everyone else: *if her father, a completely fit man, suddenly fell ill and died, and if just before falling ill he had been working with poisonous gases, then surely it was those gases which had killed him.*

The bus dipped down into a valley, and the chimney at Nancekuke disappeared from sight. From time to time they stopped to pick up small groups of waiting children, who were greeted by shouts from the back. When they came to the old house the driver automatically pulled up and Helen went forward to explain that he no longer needed to stop there. As she leant over him, there were suggestive cries from the back of the coach, and shouts of 'Watch it!' She returned to her seat, feeling that she was blushing in spite of herself, and caught only a glimpse of the walls of the old house, and its blank, empty windows.

At the top of the hill, the chimney of Nancekuke came into view again. They were drawing nearer to it all the time. She could see now a small wisp of smoke coming from the top; it looked white and innocent, and the wind was blowing it out to sea. There was never any smoke when the wind was blowing inland.

There had been no inquiry after her father's death, to establish whether there was any connection between his work and his illness. It had just been assumed that his death was due to natural causes. It seemed to Helen that this was very convenient for the authorities. It allayed any fears about the danger of the work, not only for the people involved but for all of those who lived in the neighbourhood. Her father had no longer been an employee of Nancekuke. It had all been kept very quiet.

And meanwhile her mother got no compensation, only the small pension she would have received if he had been killed in a road accident or died in any other way.

It seemed to her more than suspect. It was a great, blaring injustice.

The coach jolted into low gear, and began the descent into the next valley. This was the nearest they came to Nancekuke. A little further on a notice at a turning said: MINISTRY OF DEFENCE ESTABLISHMENT. NO THROUGH ROAD. But the school bus went off in the opposite direction, taking the road up through the valley.

This valley had once been busy with tin and copper mines, and there were several engine houses. The chimney stacks were made of stone, and tapered to the bricks around the top. They grew out of the land. They were like fingers pointing to the sky.

The chimney at Nancekuke was very different. It was a thin, whitish tube, uniform all the way up, and anchored with wire stays. It was completely alien in its landscape, sinister.

Two or three times more on the journey to school it showed up again. It was so prominent, high up on the cliffs, that it could be seen for miles. It was always there, dominating everything around it. Helen felt that she lived in its shadow.

By Wednesday evening she could stay in the house no longer. She had spent all Sunday helping to get it straight, so that her mother would not have to work on her own during the week. This meant that she had neglected her homework, and for two evenings she had been trying to bring all of this up to date. Last summer she had failed all her 'O' levels. At least, she had failed all those she took, but they had taken place when her father was in the last stages of his illness, some in the very week that he

35

died, and she had not always been at school for the exam. In fact, some she sat simply because she happened to go to school that day, without knowing whether there was an exam or not. It was a time when she had been very confused.

Now she had to pass them in November, before being allowed into the sixth form. There was a lot of work to catch up, but it was half-term that weekend, and so there was less pressure to get things finished for the next day.

As soon as tea was over, she called the dog and they left the house. She could not have studied, however necessary it might have been. She wanted to go for a long walk. She needed the monotonous rhythm of walking, and the calming effect it had on her.

She left the village and went along the western side of the headland. It was beginning to feel wintry; there was a little pale sunlight and some haze. She kept up a brisk pace, with Petra running ahead and returning to her, covering about three times the distance.

After a while she left the road and took a track down into the valley. There were dead leaves underfoot, and then a stream joined the path and overflowed it. She followed the stream until it reached another, where she took a steep path up the opposite side. This slope was very bare, covered with short, wind-cropped heather and gorse, and scarred with old mine workings. She could see the sea now, at the end of the valley.

She struggled up what had once been a mule track. The mules had taken the ore in panniers from the mines at the top to the stamps worked by water-wheels on the stream in the bottom of the valley. A mule boy would have had a team of them, going up and down all day. The girls worked at the stamps, sorting the tin. Bal maidens, they were called. The mining had stopped half a century ago, and now everything was overgrown. The valleys had returned to nature.

Helen often thought about how it had looked when the mines were working. With Tom and Alison, she had once lit a fire in the flue of a chimney, just to see the smoke coming out of the stack again. The jackdaws had flown out, cawing loudly 'What does a jackdaw say when it flies over a nudist colony?' Tom asked. 'Cor! Cor!' It had been quite exciting to see the smoke they had made billowing out.

But a hundred years ago all the chimneys were belching out smoke, the wheels turning and the stamps rattling as they crushed the ore, working day and night, becoming silent only when the streams dried up in summer.

She reached the top of the track, and paused for a moment to get her breath. Before her was a wide stretch of moorland, with a band of sea beyond. Away on one side, the chimney at Nancekuke was again visible. She turned towards the coast, intending to walk along the cliff tops back to the village.

The men, women and children had worked in terrible conditions in the mines. They had been cruelly exploited by the owners. The miners had died in rock-falls and explosions, they had been drowned when the sea broke in to their tunnels. They often worked in intense heat, and caught pneumonia when they returned to the cold and damp above ground. They worked where the air was foul, and if they survived all this the dust would get into their lungs and kill them in the end. Most of them died in the middle of their lives, just as her father had done.

But there was something dignified about their struggle to wrest minerals out of the ground. The work itself was right and proper.

And now the only chimney still smoking was that of Nancekuke. The one natural resource it was using was the ocean; apparently it needed vast quantities of water to produce lethal gas.

Through the haze, the sun was now a red ball low over the horizon. She could see the tall concrete posts of the perimeter fence, and beyond that the chimney and its cluster of buildings. Those right next to it were supported on stalk-like legs. The whole complex looked as though it was something out of science fiction. It could have been a space craft from some evil planet; it had landed on this empty moor in Cornwall, and was waiting. Then the invaders would emerge and annihilate all human life. There was no one in sight, Helen was the only person who knew. The responsibility was hers to warn mankind.

The sun was now a great ball of fire, and as she walked towards the coast she noticed that it drew steadily close to the chimney, like a guided missile homing towards its objective.

A slight change of direction in the path caused the sun to close the gap more rapidly. Helen increased her pace and away to the west the missile sun zoomed the last thousands of miles on to its target.

Helen stopped, halting the sun in its destructive course. It was still too high in the sky to touch the research station. All she had to do was wait a few minutes. She had guided it to the right point, and then 'Boum!' Nancekuke would explode.

She waited. The sun barely seemed to move. Petra returned to see why she had stopped in the middle of nowhere, then sat down to wait by her feet.

As it came closer to the earth's horizon, the sun appeared to gather momentum. It was moving visibly now, coming straight down. It seemed to grow in size. For a moment it hung poised above the chimney. Then it struck. The fireball fell upon Nancekuke, blotting it out.

Rapidly the sun slid out of sight. There was a last bit, like the clipping from a finger nail, and then it was gone.

Helen had green discs before her eyes. They gradually cleared. Everything was different, it was colder and darker now. She could see the lights of St Ives in the distance.

She was certain that Nancekuke had killed her father. It was up to her to prove it.

And to do that, she felt that she was the least suitable person in the world.

5
Improvisation

There had been times when Helen had been grateful for the monotony of school life. Arriving in the bus each morning, she had often felt glad to see the familiar old building. Its grey stones were reassuring. Life went on in the same way, nothing changed there. The same old faces in the classroom, the same old teachers, the same old lessons day after day had all been very comforting when her own life was changing, when her father was dying and when they had to move from home. It had been the one sure thing that she could cling on to in a shifting world.

But now, as the first half of the term was ending, the stability began to seem irksome. School seemed such a small, inward-looking world. It was so unreal.

As she stood in the morning assembly, just one of row upon row of identical girls, all dressed in their regulation winter uniforms, she wondered why they were there, and what it had to do with life. Outside important things were happening, things that mattered in the world. Only a few miles away from them a gas had been developed; sixty tons of it was exported every year, and no one really knew how toxic it was. Seven and a half thousand tons of it had been used in Vietnam. But this was never mentioned in school. The only thing that mattered there was the length of your skirt, and wearing the right shoes and having your hair tied back – and passing examinations.

The girls were put safely out of sight, segregated, until their childhood was over.

The reading ended, and they went down on their knees to pray. They all grumbled about this; it was uncomfortable, it ruined your tights, and it was unfair when all the members of staff just sat. But no one ever did anything about it. They all went down on their knees, and went on grumbling. Helen did the same as the rest of them, kneeling up first of all and then as that became uncomfortable going back on her heels, and all the time thinking how long it would take.

She felt that she ought to speak out, or to stand up. But she would never be able to do it, not on her own. She remained hidden in the safe anonymity of the mass.

After assembly there were a few announcements of shattering unimportance, and then they went to their form rooms to pack their satchels for the morning.

Helen was still in the fifth form, although most of her friends had gone up into the sixth, with all their privileges like not wearing school uniform.

She had had one very close friend last year, Susan, but now they were separated. She did not seem to need her so much as she used to. In the summer term she had relied upon her completely. They were still good friends, but she was more independent now.

They went off to the first lesson, which on Thursday morning was English. The room was painted two shades of green. The windows were high up, so that you could not see out; there were rows of desks crammed into the space. It was dark in the mornings now, and the room was poorly lit by three bulbs; a fourth was not working. There were one or two posters, the performance of a play in a medieval market square and Shakespeare's theatre. They had been on the walls too long, and had a tired, faded look. Girls sat around, at or on the too-small desks, chattering or calling to other groups.

The door opened and Mrs Robinson came in. The noise died away.

'Good morning, girls.'

'Good morning, Mrs Robinson,' they chanted in a depressed sort of way.

'Sit down. Take out your books of Cambridge Examination

Papers and turn to page thirteen. Here you will see a passage for summarising, and in the mock exam at the end of term, or for some of you the real exam in two or three weeks . . .'

How they loved to remind you how little time there was left! They had heard about 'O' levels since they were in the first form, and as they had gone up the school the pressure to do well had increased. They went from one harangue to another: 'You've got to work harder, you've got to learn your facts, your vocabulary, your dates, your set books. You've got to learn, you've got to work. You'll never pass, you're lazy, you don't work as well as last year's fifth.'

And now the new refrain was the mock 'O' level at the end of term. 'Mock, mock, mock,' they heard, from one lesson to the next. 'Mock, mock, mock.'

Helen did her summary of the passage about why provincial landladies no longer take theatrical lodgers. As if anyone cared! This was the second time she had summarised it anyway, and she worked quite automatically. A lot of the work she had done before. She took notes and answered questions, did exercises and problems, and made translations. And this year none of it seemed to matter. In the past she had always worked very conscientiously, but now it all seemed increasingly irrelevant. She carried on with it, as she knelt in prayers, because everyone else did, and she could not think of any alternative.

But there was one school activity which was not examinable and which for Helen had real purpose. This was the drama they had every Thursday at the boys' school after four o'clock. She looked forward to it all day.

The drama teacher had fair curly hair and a Greek profile; he was wearing a plum-red track suit, and had a cymbal suspended from one hand and a drum-stick in the other. He stepped lightly into the centre of the gymnasium, and struck with his stick. The sound rang through the hall, and the boys and girls standing in groups by the wall-bar or sitting on the vaulting boxes fell silent. A boy jumped off the trampoline. The teacher touched his cymbal, and the vibrations stopped.

'Right, let's begin!' said Colin Cordery. 'Would you come forward, fill in the spaces? There's a great gap here.'

There was some reluctance to fill it up, it seemed so exposed. Helen glanced around, then moved into the area.

'Thank you, love. Now, to begin with, a few exercises to get warmed up. Reaching up and forward as far as you can, one and two and three and four! And one and two and three and four!'

The girls had all changed into jumpers and jeans. There did not seem to be much difference between girls and boys.

'Now, rolling your shoulders, begin!'

Helen threw herself into the work. She had been allowed to join the joint sixth form drama club on the assumption that she would be a sixth former next term. At first she had been doubtful, especially about some of the things they were asked to do. Sometimes she had dropped out and watched, but as she became used to it, she enjoyed it more and more.

'Now walk around, and when I stroke the cymbal change your pace. Change your pace each time you hear the cymbal. Go!'

Helen moved around, feeling herself adjust to the direction and presence of the people about her.

'And now when you hear the cymbal change not only pace but direction as well.'

The rate at which the clashes came speeded up; it needed great concentration to keep to the instructions. Boys and girls began to fall out, laughing and breathless; there was a final loud crash on the cymbal. Everyone was now laughing. The atmosphere was very easy and relaxed.

'Good, very good!' He picked four couples in different parts of the hall. 'Now I want you to lean against each other so that you are entirely dependent on the other person for support, without him or her you would collapse. Good. Now I want the people around to join in, one by one. See where the pressures are, add your support where it's needed, but always so that you depend on the others. Build it up.'

One group collapsed, sprawling on the floor. Another milled around like a rugby scrum. There was a lot of shouting: 'Ouch! You're squashing me! Get off my feet! Quick, I'm falling! Bring some support over this side! Hurry up! I can't hold on!'

The cymbal clashed. 'Try to do it in silence. Take it quite seriously. No noise now.'

They continued, with some suppressed giggles and groans of agony. The group Helen was in was too ambitious; they tried to build upwards, the girls climbing on to the boys' shoulders, but when it reached three storeys it was too much for the base and the whole creation toppled to the ground. There was a lot of noise and laughter, and good-natured blaming of one another.

But one group was still working, and they turned to watch them. In complete silence, this group was building up a most complicated structure. It looked like the model of some molecular formula. Helen thought it was quite beautiful.

'Now try to undo it,' said Colin Cordery.

Slowly they took it apart, one by one. It was fascinating.

'Could you invent a situation which might get people into that position?'

There was a roar of laughter at the impossibility of it.

'All right, I admit it's a little unlikely. But let's have some suggestions. Anybody?'

'The first one loses some money,' a girl suggested, 'and the others come to look for it.'

'A disaster in a treacle factory, with treacle flying everywhere,' said a boy called Andy, 'and people coming to help and sticking to each other.'

'All right, will you play it that way?'

It was funny, but not so good a second time. It worked best when it had no meaning, when it was an unexplained ritual.

The cymbal clashed, a punctuation mark in the class to indicate a change of direction.

'Let's work now in pairs. Take a partner.'

Mike Launder came and stood opposite her. He always wore a long grey jersey, covered in paint; it reached almost to his knees. He wore tight jeans, and had long hair. They never had regular partners, but in the last few sessions he had worked with her. He was very good, precise and economical in his movements. Also he was more serious about it than most of the boys. He said nothing, but raised his hands to shoulder height, anticipating the next exercise. Helen placed the palms of her hands flat against his, not quite touching, and they began to move their hands as though one was a mirror image of the other with only the thickness of the glass between them. They made smooth, flowing gestures, moving very slowly and gradually extending them until they were sweeping low to the ground or reaching up to their full extent. Sometimes one led and sometimes the other; they tried to feel what their partner was going to do. Helen found it was best to do it almost instinctively. If you thought too hard about it you went wrong, but if you abandoned yourself to it and let the movements take over you could sense the pattern your hands would make. It was like dancing, in a very formal, ritualistic way; it was almost hypnotic.

The crash of the cymbal brought her out of her dream. 'I want you to work in groups, and I want you to make a protest. One minute to discuss it, three minutes to work it out. Starting now!'

Helen found herself in the same group as Mike. They talked about various protests, but from the start Mike wanted to stage a protest against the drama teacher. Helen did not think it was funny, but Mike was very urgent; it was an opportunity he was not going to miss, and he got his way.

They worked it out, with Mike doing a parody of Colin Cordery and the rest being a class turning against him. Then their time was up, and they all sat in a large circle on the floor of the gym. Each group took it in turn to perform their protest in the centre.

There was a protest against noise, with different people imitating different sources of noise, cars, motor-bikes and aircraft, beginning quietly and working up to a scream.

'Good,' said Colin. 'A stench in the ears! What have we got next?'

The next was a protest against protests. A crowd was waving banners, chanting and singing, but when they were questioned they thought the demonstration was against a whole variety of things, or they did not know what it was about at all.

'I protest!' shouted Mike, before they had finished. 'The Young Conservatives of the sixth form, dirty reactionaries –'

He had stood up, and those around him tried to pull him down, grabbing his jumper and stretching it to his ankles. Others got hold of him and brought him to the floor, smothering his words. Occasional shouts could be heard – 'bourgeois ... totalitarian methods ... silence the opposition' before they were muffled again.

'Do you think they've got a point?' asked Colin, when the brawl had subsided.

'No!' bawled Mike, breaking free again.

'We've heard you, let's hear someone else.'

'No,' said Helen. 'I don't.'

'Why not?'

'Well, it might be true of some people. But it needs courage to stand up for what you think is right.'

'Courage? Isn't it easy in a crowd?'

'It's not always in a crowd. Sometimes the crowd's against you, and you've got to persuade them. That's not easy, that's going against the crowd. It's easy to sit back and do nothing.'

'But it's fun making a demonstration, isn't it? Don't you think a lot are doing it for the fun of demonstrating? Don't you think this group makes a fair point?'

Helen shook her head.

'Come on, let's see your group having fun.' He must have seen something of their preparations.

'I don't believe in it,' said Helen. 'I'm only acting.'

'I'm not,' said Mike.

Colin laughed, ready to enjoy it. They stood around, as at the beginning of a class. Mike borrowed the cymbal and stick, and pranced into the middle, rolling his hips and patting the back of his hair. 'Come along, darlings!' he said, giving the cymbal a bang. 'Reach up to the sky. And one and two and three and four! Now, roll those hips!'

It was cruel. Helen felt that Mike should not be doing this.

Gradually the class stopped working, and began to chant, very quietly at first, 'Down with Colin Cordery.' Then as it got louder they began to stamp their feet to the rhythm, and then to march. 'Down with Colin Cordery.' They marched around the circle, and broke through to march around the hall.

'Come on, everyone join in!' called Colin, and he led the rest on to the end of the procession, and now they were all parading and stamping and shouting. 'Down with Colin Cordery.'

Helen's feet slammed against the floor, she gave herself to the rhythm. 'Down with Colin Cordery.' Dum, dum, dumty dum diddy. It was intoxicating and a bit frightening, the feeling of power it gave you. It was like being possessed. 'Down with Colin Cordery.'

The column came back to the centre, the chanting faded away, and they flopped down exhausted.

'Enter the headmaster,' said Colin. 'But it proves my point. You demonstrate for fun, whether you mean it or not.'

'We meant it,' said Mike.

And even Helen, who had not meant it, had to admit that during the marching she had felt as though she had meant it. If she had been given a knife then, and the chanting had turned to 'Kill him! Kill him!' and they had all plunged their knives in, she could not be certain that she would not have been amongst them.

Colin just laughed. He did not seem to mind the protest at all. 'After all this excitement, let's relax. Lie flat on the floor. Become aware of your right-hand big toe. Let it relax. And let it fall off. Now the other toes, one by one. Let them fall off.'

46

Very slowly, he went over the whole body, until every part of it had fallen away. It was a lovely feeling at the end; Helen felt completely eased.

'And now, as you breathe out, let the breath come out with a noise. Nobody's listening to you personally, it can be any noise, whatever comes.'

Gradually the sounds began, strange weird noises like souls in an inferno. Baritone, tenor and contralto sounds were sustained in a chorus; new sounds suddenly blared out. Helen was only partly aware of them. It was extraordinary, she seemed to be floating. She felt free.

'And that's all we've time for today,' said Colin quietly. 'See you next week, have a good half term!'

She returned to earth, and went to the back of the hall to fetch her coat, satchel and the flower-printed paper carrier in which she had her school uniform. Goodbye cries echoed across the gym. Colin was putting his cymbal into a round case. She wondered where he lived. She felt he folded himself away in another case until the next drama lesson.

6
The Journalist

When they had been clearing and sorting at the old house (for years of living there had produced such an accumulation that much had to be thrown away), Helen had found an old black felt hat with a wide, floppy brim. She had carefully put it aside and made sure it went with the rest of her clothes to the new house. On Saturday morning, when she was getting ready to go shopping with Paul, she took it out and placed it on her head. She zipped Paul into his anorak.

'Goodbye then,' she said, opening the kitchen door. 'We're just going.'

'God!' exclaimed Alison. 'What are you wearing?'

'Do you like it?'

'No, you look like a witch.'

'Which witch?' said Tom.

'Helen, are you trying to be a hippy?' asked her mother.

'Don't be silly!'

'But you aren't going out like that, are you?'

'Of course I am.'

'Well, I don't know —'

'I like it.'

She felt very attached to it. She wanted to wear it very much, it was quite important. She had found something she could wear which did not become commonplace once she put it on, even if she was wearing it with her old navy blue duffel coat.

There was a noise at the door, and two letters came through the box. Helen was nearest, and picked them up. One was for her, addressed in a handwriting she did not recognise.

Mr Wyatt! she thought, and at once felt anxious, in case she should not have written. In the middle of the week she had half expected a letter, but when nothing arrived she had given up thinking of a reply.

She gave her mother the circular, and opened hers, wishing she could read it privately. It was only a short note.

Dear Helen,

Very shocked to learn your news, which I hadn't heard, and deeply grateful to you for letting me know. I can't begin to say how sorry I am. I'm coming to Cornwall this weekend and should arrive tomorrow, Saturday, late afternoon. Hoping to see you then,

Sincerely,

Bill Wyatt

'Who's it from?' asked her mother.

'Mr Wyatt.'

'Who's Mr Wyatt?'

'Do you know him?'

'I've never heard of him.'

'He was someone Dad knew, a friend of his.'

'I knew all his friends. He didn't know anyone called Wyatt.'

'Are you sure he never mentioned him?'

'Never.'

Mrs Roberts looked alarmed, she did not like the unexpected. She seemed suspicious, as though something upsetting was going to happen. 'Why is he writing to you?' she asked.

'I wrote to him.'

'Whatever for?'

'Dad gave me his address. I thought he wanted me to.'

'I don't understand it, your father would have told me. What does he say?'

'He's coming this afternoon.' She handed her mother the letter.

'Oh no! I hope he doesn't expect to stay the night, I can't possibly put him up.'

'Don't worry, Mum! He would have said –'

'I'll have to offer him a meal, though I don't know what I shall give him. We don't know what time he's coming.'

'You needn't bother.'

'But what does he want? We don't mean anything to him, and to come all this way! I wish you hadn't written, Helen. You should have told me.

'It's all right! I'll get everything ready. I'll go now.'

'You aren't going like that, are you?'

'Why not?'

'But, Helen, it looks so — eccentric.'

'You look mad,' said Alison.

Helen pulled the hat down over her eyes and ears. Now she really looked mad, though for her it was an impression of the house they lived in.

'You're sick, kid,' said Alison.

'What do you get when you put lunar sand in a clock,' said Tom. 'A lunatic!'

Helen fetched the shopping bag and purse, put Paul in his push-chair, and set off for the shops. As she walked, the brim of the hat flopped up and down, and the rhythm of it got into her step. She bounced along.

As the day went on, Mrs Roberts grew more and more agitated. After dinner she dressed, looking smarter than she had for almost a year. A high tea of ham and salad was on the table by four o'clock. Helen changed into a dress. They had no more to do but wait for his arrival.

Alison was riding as usual, and Tom was in a friend's house on the estate. Paul was tired, and had taken his dummy and the blanket he always cuddled when he wanted comforting into the living room, and lay back in an easy chair watching sports on television. It was the nearest he ever came to having a sleep in the day.

Helen made some tea, and they drank it in the kitchen, to be on their own. Suddenly Paul came rushing in, trailing the long blue blanket along the floor behind him.

'I see my daddy on television,' he shouted. 'I see my daddy.'

There was an awful silence.

'It couldn't be, dear,' said Mrs Roberts.

'Yes, I see my daddy.'

He had not mentioned his father since the weeks immediately after his death. They hurried into the living room, to satisfy themselves as much as the child. On the screen a few small figures were running up and down.

'You were dreaming, dear.' She stroked his head.

'Is my daddy dead?'

'Yes, dear.'

'Why my daddy dead?'

'He wasn't very well, darling. He went to hospital, but they couldn't make him better.'

'Couldn't make him better?'

'No, usually they make people better. But they couldn't make him better.'

'Mummy.'

'Yes.'

'Where my daddy is?'

She hesitated a moment. 'In heaven, darling.'

'In Devon?'

'No, darling. In Heaven.'

Helen felt confused, as much as the child. She had once accepted religious beliefs unquestioningly, but now she did not know. She could not really believe in a heaven. She waited for his next question. Where would her mother say heaven was? She did not think her mother's faith was very certain, it was more conventional. But Paul asked no more.

She settled him in the chair again with his blanket, and they returned to their unfinished cups of tea.

'I wonder why he suddenly thought of that.'

'I expect he fell asleep.'

'Mother, before Mr Wyatt comes,' said Helen, 'there are some things I'd like to ask you.'

'What about?'

'About Dad.'

She could feel the reluctance come down like a barrier.

'What is it?'

'Why did he really die?'

'He had leukaemia.'

'Yes, I know. But how did he get that?'

'I don't know any more about it than you do.'

'But don't you think that's just the sort of thing poison gas would cause? Before he died, didn't he say —'

'Nothing, I know nothing,' her mother said in exasperation. 'I don't know any more than you, I wish you'd leave me alone. First Paul, and then you. And now you've got this Mr Wyatt coming, and we'll go over it all again. Leave me alone!'

In tears, she ran from the room. Helen felt sorry, and ashamed that she had made her mother cry, but stubbornly did not regret asking her questions, and knew that she would ask them again.

Her mother remained upstairs, so that when there was a knock at the door, it was Helen who answered. The man standing on the doorstep was tall and wore a sheepskin driving coat. He was much younger than she had expected. She had thought a friend of her father's would be about his age; William Wyatt seemed to be in his mid-twenties. He had a lot of hair, thick-rimmed glasses and a little wispy beard on his chin.

'Helen Roberts?' he asked, holding out his hand. 'I'm Bill Wyatt.'

She shook his hand. 'Come in.'

'I hope it's all right my turning up like this, I'm sorry I couldn't give you more warning.'

'That's all right. My mother should be down in a moment.' Helen hoped she would not refuse to meet Mr Wyatt; she did not want to have to entertain him entirely on her own. Paul had gone upstairs too, so the living room was empty. 'She's resting at the moment with my young brother.'

'How many of you are there?'

He could not have been a very close friend if he did not know that. She told him all about the family, and he asked more questions about them, not as though he was making conversation but as though he really wanted to know. As they talked she had the extraordinary feeling that she had met him before; she was sure she had seen him somewhere, but she could not place where it was.

After a while, when he had found out a lot about their family and where they used to live, and she had found out nothing about his connection with her father, she asked him if he was hungry and he said he'd rather wait for the family to come in. She offered him a drink and he said he would love a cup of coffee as he had driven from London with only one brief stop. He had done the journey in five hours, which was fast going.

She went to the kitchen to make the coffee, and he followed. He left his coat in the hall. She liked his choice of clothes, a dark roll-neck sweater, cord trousers slightly flared, suede boots. He found cups, milk and sugar, moving around the kitchen as though he was quite at home. She thought he was used to being in strange houses; it always took her a long time to adapt to new surroundings. He was casual and relaxed, chatting all the time; he was very easy to get on with. Helen found it very pleasant, making coffee together.

So she was not very pleased when Tom came in to be noticed.

'Is that your car?' he asked. This was what had brought him in, a bright orange sports car parked outside the house. Bill Wyatt gave all his attention to Tom, and talked about cars and fishing.

'Have you caught anything?'

'Only a cod with an "I" in.'

'An eel?'

'No, an "l".'

'A cold,' explained Helen, wearily.

Tom fetched his guitar. Bill Wyatt admired it, tuned it up and tried it out.

'Your coffee's getting cold,' she pointed out.

'Yes, thanks.' He took a few gulps, and continued playing.

She looked at him, with his head bent over the guitar, very absorbed in what he was doing. His brown hair fell over his glasses, the light shone through the pale hairs on his chin. He did not play badly.

'I'm sure I've seen you before,' she said.

He looked up and grinned. 'On the box, perhaps,' he said, nodding towards the set in the corner.

Yes, that was it! But what was the programme?

'Are you on television?' asked Tom, enormously impressed. 'Are you famous? Do you play in a group?'

He laughed uproariously. 'No, this is only a hobby!'

Then Alison made her entry, and she and Tom kept reeling off the names of television personalities, mixing up real people and fictitious characters, and asking him if he knew them, and he answered good humouredly that he did or did not. Alison flirted like mad, and before long he had promised to drive her to the youth club in his sports car.

Helen went up to see her mother. She was lying on her bed, with the curtains drawn.

'Are you coming down, Mum?'

'What does he want?'

'I don't know. He wants to see you.'

'I can't see any reason for it. We have nothing for him, and he has nothing for us. It's not necessary.'

'You won't know if you don't meet him. Come on, Mum. We all want our tea.'

Reluctantly, she got up, tidied her clothes and re-did her make-up. She and Paul followed Helen to the living room.

As soon as they entered, Bill Wyatt jumped to his feet. 'Mrs Roberts,' he said, taking her hand. 'I was so sorry to hear about your husband. I wish I had known sooner, I'm afraid I can't be of much use now. I didn't know Tom very well, I only met him the once. But I knew his work. . . .'

He was trying to charm their mother, as he had charmed

them all, one by one. And Helen could see her mother resisting his influence, still suspicious of him.

Yet the meal was one of the happiest they had had for a long time. Mealtimes were usually dreadful, with everyone in their worst moods, and not caring. With Bill there, they all seemed to relax. Instead of shovelling food back in order to get away as quickly as possible, they took their time. It was not what they said, none of it was very memorable. But they enjoyed talking and listening, and they laughed a lot.

'Why do you have two cups, Paul?' Bill asked.

'One for slow drinks,' said Paul. 'And one for quick drinks.' He gave a demonstration.

Helen suddenly saw what to them was quite normal with an outsider's eyes, and it seemed eccentric and funny.

Tom kept on telling jokes and no one tried to shut him up. Each joke in itself was terribly unfunny, but when one succeeded the other they seemed to become funny and in the end they were laughing at anything, Bill the loudest of all.

'A burglar was passing a police station and there was a notice "Wanted for shopbreaking" and he thought, "Good, I'll apply for that!" . . . an aeroplane was flying over a desert island and there was "rescue me" spelt out on it in stones, and the pilot turned to his co-pilot and said, "That's a funny name for an island" . . . A monkey was born without kneecaps. His mother didn't have very much money, but she took what she had to the zoo and asked if they had two ape-knees for a penny. Do you get it? Two ha'pennies –'

'Yes, we get it all right.'

'He gets them all out of *Beano* and *Dandy*.'

'Mummy always read *Sunny Stories* when she was a girl.'

'She was a very goody-goody little girl. I bet when her mummy said, "Come along, Jean. It's time for bed," she would answer, "All right Mummy, coming!" '

But their mother did not respond to this teasing; she said nothing.

'I hate books where the children go to bed at seven o'clock.

And where they have nannies. And where they are always very good.'

'And where they always manage to do so much. They come to Cornwall and in ten minutes they find the clue to the sunken treasure ship, and all the locals haven't found it in hundreds of years!'

'I can't stand magicky books. I like books to be real.'

'*How to Climb Mount Everest*,' said Tom. 'By Will E. Doit. Illustrated by E. Wont.' And he began to reel off a number of joke book titles. '*Pony Riding* by Jim Khana. *Droopy Drawers* by Loopy Lastic. *Winter Sports* by Bob Sleigh.'

They greeted each with groans.

'*Chemical Warfare* by Nancy Kuke.'

After this one, there was silence. Bill tried to start another subject, but failed. The meal was over. Alison left to get dressed. The others remained around the table.

'Mr Wyatt, what do you do?' asked their mother.

'I write.'

'Do you write books?'

'No, scientific articles, mostly.'

'Are you a journalist?'

'Yes, you could call it that, I suppose.'

Helen remembered the programme in which she had seen him. It was to do with a conference on germ and chemical warfare, and he had been interviewed about it. She was sure he had been interviewed, and not the other way round.

'There's nothing interesting about us,' said her mother nervously. 'You aren't going to write about us, are you?'

'No, of course not.'

'Then why did you come here?'

'I came because Helen wrote to me.'

'It's a long way to come.'

'I'm not after a story, honestly.'

'There isn't one here, you know. I haven't got anything to tell.'

'I quite understand.'

'I'm sorry you've come such a long way for nothing, but we can't help you.'

'I only wanted to know if I could help you.'

'There's nothing we need, we're quite all right, thank you.'

At that moment Alison returned to show herself off, wearing her white skinnyrib, which left a bare midriff showing above the top of her cords. Bill Wyatt stood up. 'I promised to drop Alison off at her youth club.'

'You aren't driving back to London straight away?' Helen asked.

'No, I've booked at the hotel for the night, I'll be going back tomorrow.'

'But you can't go yet!' she exclaimed. 'We haven't said anything.'

'There's nothing to say,' said her mother. She got up and began almost mechanically to complain about what Alison was wearing, following her out to see that she put on something warm.

'But there must be,' said Helen. 'You must have something to tell us. You must know something about our Dad.'

'It's no good. Your mother is determined not to talk about it. Could I talk to you some time?'

'Where?'

They broke off as Mrs Roberts returned, and they continued stacking the plates. They found themselves alone together a few moments later in the kitchen.

'I'll be outside the hotel at eight o'clock,' he said. 'Can you make it?'

She nodded. They had almost cleared the living room table when Alison flounced in, impatient at being kept waiting. 'I'm ready,' she announced, throwing back her hair and showing her profile. It was all a great performance, taken from old films on television.

'The carriage awaits.' He bowed low, and Alison swept out. It was a bit ridiculous, thought Helen, from a teeny-bopper like Alison, and then before she reached the front door, Tom said, 'I'm coming in the car.'

'No you aren't!'

'I am. He said so.'

'You little liar! He said I was the only one.'

'He said I could come too.'

'If you come in the car, I'm warning you –'

And they were at it, cat and dog.

William Wyatt said his farewells as though he'd received a most cordial welcome. 'It was a lovely meal. I'm so glad everything's all right. If you ever want me . . .'

Then he was gone, the sports car roaring down the road with Alison triumphant and Tom running down the pavement.

Helen could not wait to get to her mother. 'Really, how could you be so rude? He was a friend of father's and he came all this way, to be treated like that!'

'I don't trust him.'

'Well, I do.'

'He only came for his own ends.'

'I wrote to him.'

'He couldn't have come from London for that. He came snooping around. He wanted to pry into our lives.'

'That's not fair, Mother!'

'I know what they do, these journalists. They try to get you to open your hearts to them, and then they publish it for the whole world to read.'

'He's not like that.'

'He was just after a story.'

'Mother, we haven't got anything to hide. We haven't got any secrets.'

'I don't want it in the papers, that's all. I don't want it talked about.'

'But why not? I think it's best for everything to be in the open. I think if there's anything at all suspicious about the way Father died, then it's best to discuss it, not to try and hush it up.'

'It's all over. It won't do any good to investigate, and go into it all again. It only makes trouble.'

'We must know the truth – that's important.'

'It's all in the past, and it's best left there.'

'The way you speak, you make it seem as though there is something to cover up.'

'There isn't. I've told you all I know. I don't know any more.'

'But Dad must have thought about it himself, he must have known whether it was the gas or not. Didn't he ever say –'

'He never said anything about it.'

'Then why did he give me Bill Wyatt's address?'

'That I don't understand at all.'

'He must have wanted us to get in touch with him.'

'Perhaps he was confused.'

'That's not true. He was tired, but his mind was perfectly clear.'

'He said one or two odd things.'

'Such as?'

'I can't remember.'

'But this is exactly what you have to remember. It might seem odd to us, but it might be a clue to what really happened. What did he say, Mother?'

'I don't know, it was nothing. I really can't remember.'

'Oh Mother, I give up.'

'It doesn't do any good to worry about it, it's over.'

Helen gave a gesture of despair. Her mother was hopeless, she did not understand. 'I can't stay in this evening,' she said. 'I'm going out.'

'Where are you going?'

'Youth club, I suppose. Where else is there?'

7
The German Shell

The Miners' Arms was the only three-storey building in the village, an old Georgian inn on one side of the small square opposite the church. In front of the hotel, Helen could see the orange sports car, but there was no sign of Bill. As she drew near she realised he was sitting inside. He leant across to open the door for her, and she slipped into the front seat without anyone having seen her.

Doubt about whether she should be doing this crossed her mind. Her mother said she did not trust him. He was almost a stranger, and here she was getting into his car and she had no idea where they were going. But she was determined to find out what he knew. And her father had trusted him.

'I like your hat,' he said. 'It's great!'

Helen was pleased.

'Now, where shall we go? Where can we talk? Somewhere like a coffee bar, perhaps?'

She suggested one in a small port further along the coast, where there would be no one from the village or the school to recognise her. 'If it's not too far,' she added. 'You've driven a long way already today.'

'No, I like driving.'

He started the car, and they moved smoothly away, the headlights sweeping along the grey faces of the houses. Soon they were out of the village and on the coast road.

'I'm sorry my mother was so rude to you,' Helen apologised. 'I didn't expect her to behave like that.'

'I suppose she wants to forget.'

'I want to know.'

'What do you want to know?'

'I want to know if my father was killed by poison gas.'

'It's quite possible.'

'How can I find out?'

'Are you sure you want to? Perhaps your mother's right – it won't make any difference.'

'But it will! Because then we would know the truth. And if he was killed by the gas, then it would show people that it *is* dangerous.'

Bill did not answer for a moment, as he changed gear to take a sharp bend on a hill. Then he said, 'Yes, I feel like you. I didn't think your mother would be so up-tight about it.'

'It's a sort of loyalty. Dad never spoke about his work, even to her, and so she feels she mustn't say anything about it now.'

'Does she get any compensation?'

'No, only the widow's pension.'

'She could claim that it was an industrial injury. What I should like to do is to write an article drawing attention to your mother's position, suggesting a possible connection between your father's work and his death, and calling for an inquiry.'

'Mum wouldn't support it.'

'It's to her own benefit. Could you persuade her?'

Helen felt very doubtful, and shook her head.

'Would you tell me all you remember about your father from the first symptoms of his illness until his death – I should be able at least to say if it definitely was not gas poisoning. You don't mind talking about it?'

'No, I want to. Mother never will, and there isn't anyone else.'

So Helen started with her father's visit to Germany, because it was about a month after this that he came home from work one day with a headache and feeling very dizzy and hot. He had thought it was flu, and that he had a temperature, but from then on he was rarely free of headaches and dizziness and various aches and pains. One day he had been walking to the front gate when he had fallen over, crashing down on to the

61

lawn. It had been very alarming to see him collapse like this, and from then on they knew he was seriously ill. He never went back to work again after that.

From time to time she interrupted her story to tell Bill which road to take, and before she had finished they arrived in the town. He parked on the sea front, and she stepped from the warm luxury of the car on to the windswept promenade. Away in the dark, invisible waves were roaring, and spray blew through the air. They hurried into an out-of-season café, the only one remaining open.

'We could go to a pub if you like,' said Bill. 'I suppose you're old enough.'

'No, let's stay here.'

She sat on a bench seat against the wall, with a mural of bright blue sea and shell-covered sand behind her. Bill fetched two coffees, and sat opposite her, leaning forward on the table. A juke box was playing at the back of the café.

'When he was ill, did he suffer from convulsions at all?' Bill asked.

'Yes, one arm shook all the time. He kept going into hospital for a few days for tests and blood transfusions, and then coming home. He would be quite well for a while after having blood, except for the twitches in his arm, and then he would begin to get very tired again. His face became very drawn. He had to go back to hospital more and more frequently. But he could go for walks when he wasn't too bad, right up to the last week. He enjoyed that. I used to walk with him when I could. He often used to stop and sit down. Once he stretched out in the heather and went fast asleep. I was very frightened, I just waited for him to wake up. After about ten minutes he went on talking as though nothing had happened, I don't think he knew he had been to sleep. Often he would stop not because he was tired, but just to look around and take it all in. I didn't know at the time, but looking back at it now I can see he knew he was looking at it for the last time. And he found it all so beautiful, so painfully beautiful – you could see it in his eyes.'

Helen found that she was crying.

Bill put his hand over the back of hers on the table; she had been twisting the wrapper from the sugar into shreds. 'You've had a tough time, Helen,' he said.

'Do you think it was the gas?'

'It could be. It's very like the symptoms of nerve gas poisoning.'

'They said it was a brain tumour, and then fibrositis and epilepsy, and finally they called it leukaemia. I don't think they really knew.'

'There's a pamphlet published by the World Health Organisation which describes the effects of nerve gas – I'll check the details when I get back, but I'm sure they correspond very closely.'

'Is there anything else I can tell you?' asked Helen.

'No, let me tell you now what I know.' He moved closer to her. 'I met your father in London on his way back from Germany. I knew what he was doing there. Some wartime gas shells had been discovered, and there was no record of what they contained, but it was thought they had been developed at the end of the war. The Germans had a huge stockpile of Tabun, and this was either Sarin, of which they had about half a ton, or their first research into V-agents.'

'Did he tell you this?'

'No, I'd found out from other sources. He'd been to Germany to have a look at these shells, and make arrangements for one to be transported to England for him to work on.'

'He must have started on it and then fell ill.'

'Those bombs were old and corroded. They were in a very dangerous state. But if there had been any accident your father would have recorded it.'

'Perhaps it had seemed slight.'

'No, I think your father would have recorded even the slightest thing, in self-defence. After all, he knew it could deprive himself or his family of compensation.'

'He was always very exact.'

63

'Which leaves two possibilities, supposing he was working on the German bomb. There could have been some sort of leakage of which he was not aware. Or, of course, the leukaemia was developing quite independently.'

'It's so convenient for them to call it leukaemia,' said Helen bitterly. 'It stops people from getting alarmed about what goes on there.' She finished her coffee; she had drunk the rest without being aware of it. 'I can't understand how my father could do such work,' she added.

'I thought he regretted it,' said Bill. 'He didn't say much, but when I met him I was reporting a scientific meeting and he came up and said he wanted to meet me. He said he had read some of the pamphlets I've written for AGA – Anti-Gas Action. Then he said jokingly, but a bit defensively I thought, that he was one of "the enemy". And after we had talked for a while, he said, "I don't think you're wrong. If I were younger – " and he left it at that.'

'I think that must be why he gave me your address. He wanted me to know your point of view.'

'More than that,' said Bill. 'I imagine your father gave you my address to draw our attention to his case. He knew he was dying, and he wanted to make sure that he wouldn't be conveniently forgotten. He couldn't find out any more for himself, he was no longer able to work there, so he was passing it on to us. We've got to try and get an inquiry opened. We've got to produce all the evidence we can to show that your father died because of his work. We've got to get your mother full compensation. We've got to take up this case and fight it on his behalf. And this is what AGA is for.'

He looked into her eyes. 'It's what your father wanted, Helen. We've got to carry on his fight.'

They left the café. It was blowing hard outside, and waves were breaking over the wall. They hurried into the car, shivering, and slamming doors quickly. Helen tried to fasten her safety belt, and could not manage it. It kept falling apart. She got confused. Bill laughed, and leaning across fixed it for her.

64

'Come on!' he said. 'Let's go and have a look at the enemy citadel. The stronghold of the forces of evil. The dark power in our midst. Nancekuke.'

'Have you ever seen it before?'

'No. I went around Porton when they opened it to journalists. But Nancekuke remains unvisited, the black and secret kingdom of the trolls. I've been wanting to have a look at it for a long time – your letter gave me the excuse to come down.'

They passed one of the notices: MINISTRY OF DEFENCE ESTABLISHMENT. NO THROUGH ROAD. The lane wound up a steep hill, flattening out as they came to the top of the cliffs. Ahead of them the road was barred by a high iron gate; it stood out in the headlights of the car, and the wire fence on concrete posts stretched away into the darkness on either side.

Bill drove right up to the gates and stopped; he dipped the lights, and switched off the engine. The wind howled around the car. The gates looked old and rusted, with barbed wire woven around them. There was a notice board, and the paint had almost faded away. Beyond the gates it was dark and empty; there were no lights, no signs of life, just a feeling of nothingness.

'It's extraordinary,' said Bill, 'the thinking behind it. It's not real, it's a fantasy. It's all worked out in terms of a fairytale. The thorn hedge around a sleeping princess, a magic droplet with the power to kill every living person in the country, the secret kingdom perched like an eyrie high up on a remote and wild coast. It's a land of castles and giants and goblins, and fantastic evil powers. It belongs to magic, and the horrifying thing is that it's real, a nightmare that comes true.'

Helen felt afraid, and yet excited. 'Do you think they'll come out?' she asked.

'No, but they're watching us! Their little beady eyes are glued to their radar screens, waiting to see our next move. They are on the alert, their motor-cycles are ready to come zooming down on us. They've switched on the secret microphones to pick up our conversation, the tape recorders have started to turn.'

'Bill, I'm frightened.'

'Right, I'll give them a salute, and then we'll go.'

He flashed his headlights three times, quite slowly and deliberately. The road along the moors behind the barrier disappeared into the darkness. The whole place seemed deserted, just the remains of an old airfield from the last war. No one knew they were there, and no one cared.

Bill wound down the window on his side. The wind was loud, and came gusting into the car. He leant out and called at the top of his voice, 'Is there anybody there?'

The words were snatched away by the wind.

Then he wound up the window, started the engine, backed very fast, turned and drove off.

'They're coming,' he said. 'The motor-cyclists have left. Did you hear their engines?'

'You're making it up!'

'Don't you believe it! They knew we were there all right.'

They were away, down the hill, and then fast up the valley, the road like a winding black river rushing towards them. Helen began to feel safe again.

'It's incredible, isn't it?' he said. 'A well-organised gang or a private army ought to be able to take that place over. And it contains enough gas to poison every man, woman and child in the country. What are the Cornish Nationalists doing?' He went on to talk about the different nerve gases and their effects. 'And they say it's all done for the sake of defence. What defence, for heaven's sake! They haven't even issued gas masks, as they did at the beginning of the last war. Because they know there isn't any defence. You can't protect a whole population from these new gases, so why produce them?'

He glanced at Helen. 'I'm sorry, going on like this.'

'No, I want to hear it.'

'We need some fresh air, to blow it all out of our minds. Is there a beach we could walk on?'

'Yes, if you like.'

'But what time do you have to be in? I'm not keeping you out too late, am I?'

'That's all right.'

'Then show me the way.'

They had nearly reached the village, but instead of going into the main street, they turned off along the road to the single cove on the western, exposed side of the headland. The car glided down the narrow road cut into the steep side of the valley, with the hill above and a sheer, unfenced drop below. At the bottom the headlights of the car swung on to the sea. It was all white, a great turmoil of breaking waves within the two arms of the cove.

He left the lights shining across the churning expanse of water, and they could see to pick their way over the rocks and pebbles. Two enormous shadows were cast ahead of them, and the wind was whipping the tops off the waves and sending it flying in lumps of foam. Part of the beach was covered in this froth, and the wind blew it into their faces and away inland. It was difficult to stand upright. He took her hand in his.

The tide was almost in, and so there was no sand to walk on. They stood watching the waves thundering on to the rocks; the wind seemed to cut through their clothes as though they were made of paper.

'Look, there's someone in the water!' Helen screamed in order to be heard.

'They must be mad!'

A head was bobbing about in the surf, disappearing under the waves and emerging again in the trough behind the crest.

'Come on! He must be in trouble.'

They stumbled along the pebbles and rocks of the beach, sometimes losing sight of the dark shape struggling in the foaming water, until they reached the point nearest to the swimmer. The figure was now floundering about near the edge, but still not rising to its feet.

'What is it?' shouted Bill.

Helen suddenly realised. 'It's a seal!'

A wave threw it on to the beach, and the water sucked back through the pebbles into the sea. They ran down to it.

'Is it all right?'

'I don't think so.' It must have been injured, otherwise it would not have been washed up.

Its head was like a dog's, with big, pained eyes. Then they had to move back as the next wave swept in, shifting the seal like a bundle of seaweed.

When they went near it again they saw that its body was quivering. The tail threshed violently from side to side, until once more a wave tumbled the animal along the rocks.

'It's ill!'

'What can we do?'

'We couldn't shift it on our own. Has it got any injuries?'

They approached it warily, and Bill tried to turn it over but it lashed out with its body. As far as they could see in the light from the car headlamps, its skin and fur was thick enough to withstand the battering it was getting on the shore. But behind its neck was a brownish patch, as though it had been singed.

'Look, it's been burnt!' said Bill.

Again they had to retreat before the oncoming wave, which floated the seal, until the next rush of water brought it crashing back on to the rocks. It lay twitching and jerking.

'There's nothing we can do,' said Bill. 'It can't survive this for very long.'

They went back to the car, where it was easier to talk.

'Couldn't we phone the RSPCA?' asked Helen. 'They often look after seals, there's a sanctuary in the next cove. They've taken a lot in this last week.'

Bill looked up. 'You say there have been a lot of seals washed ashore?'

'Yes, in the last few days.'

'Where?'

'All around here.'

'But only on the north coast?'

'As far as I know.'

'I wonder,' said Bill. 'Do you think there could be any connection? Have you heard anyone suggest that it might have something to do with Nancekuke?'

'No.'

'It's very odd, seals dying in the sea around Nancekuke. I'm going to ring the RSPCA.'

Late as it was, he was able to get in touch with an official who confirmed that thirty-five dead or dying seals had been washed ashore along ten miles of the north coast in the last week. He had been visiting all the coves and beaches, either putting them out of their misery or transporting them to the seal sanctuary if it seemed that they had a chance of surviving.

Helen had gone into the call box with Bill. 'Can he do anything for our seal?' she asked.

Bill got him to promise to visit the cove the following morning.

'How are they dying?' Bill asked.

It semed that many of them had burn marks, as though they had been in contact with acid. It was not known that any ship had lost or leaked such a cargo. Bill put down the receiver.

'I'll get this into Monday's edition,' he said.

'You won't be able to say it has anything to do with Nancekuke.'

'No, I shall just give the facts about the seals dying, and then I shall say "In the centre of this coastline is Nancekuke, the government factory supplying one of the most deadly of conventional weapons, nerve gas." And the readers can draw their own conclusions.'

He seemed very satisfied.

'The poor seals!' said Helen.

'I wonder if I can get a photographer to take some pictures of them. And I want you to take me to the seal sanctuary tomorrow. Will you meet me at nine o'clock?'

Helen agreed.

'And now I'd better get you home, or your mum will be

getting worried.'

They had to get out of the car to clean the windscreen, which was all gummed up with the foam blowing off the sea. It was too sticky for the wipers to clean, and Bill rubbed away at it with a cloth, though he was not completely successful.

Helen took a last look around. The deserted cove, the light across the water, Nancekuke up on the cliffs and the injured seal lying on the beach, it all gave her a feeling of excitement. Things were happening, and she was involved in them. There was a strange sense that what they were doing was secret, even illegal.

'It's like being smugglers or wreckers,' she said, as they got back into the car.

'Yes, wreckers,' said Bill. 'I like that.'

They drove back with the wipers going. He stopped at the end of the road to the estate.

'See you tomorrow.'

'Yes.'

'And try and persuade your mother to change her mind.'

'I'll try.'

'Thanks a lot.' He put his arm around her shoulder, and gave it a squeeze. 'You're a brave kid,' he said. She did not like the 'kid' very much.

A few moments later she was running through the street towards home.

Her mother was waiting up for her.

'Look at the time, it's gone eleven o'clock,' she began, as though she had been working up to this point for quite a while. 'Where have you been? Don't tell me you've been to the youth club, because Alison came in over an hour ago! What have you been doing since then?'

'It's all right, Mum.'

'It's not all right. You can't tell me it's all right, coming in as late as this. Where have you been?'

'There's nothing to worry about.'

'You ought to be in by ten o'clock. Of course I shall worry if you're late and I don't know where you are. I'm bound to worry.'

'I'm sorry.'

'Ten o'clock is quite reasonable, but I must know where you are, Helen. It's only fair to me, isn't it? I was imagining all sorts of things.'

'I didn't go to the youth club.'

'Then where were you?'

'I went out with Bill.'

'Oh, Helen, how could you! Really, I didn't think you'd do a thing like that, you've always been so sensible. He's far too old for you to go out with.'

'He's all right, Mum.'

'You ought to have friends of your own age. I've always wanted you to mix with young people more. He's too old.'

'He's interesting.'

'What's he thinking of, going out with sixteen-year-old girls? He might be married for all you know.'

'I've no idea. I just like talking to him – or listening, rather,' she added.

'He wouldn't have done it if your father had been alive. He's taking advantage of us.'

'No, he's not like that.'

'He's a troublemaker.'

'Well, you've got to make trouble sometimes. If things are wrong, you'll never put them right without causing some trouble.'

'Is this what he's been telling you? I don't want any trouble, and he's come here to stir it up. You shouldn't listen to him, you should form your own ideas.'

'That is my own idea.'

'I suppose you were alone with him in his car all evening.'

'We went to a coffee bar.'

'I don't like this being alone, it's too dangerous. I'd rather you were at the youth club.'

'You ought to see what goes on at the youth club, Mother!' Helen retorted. 'You ought to see Alison there with her boy-friends, and she's only twelve!'

'I don't mind if they're all in one room together, and there's someone keeping an eye on them. It's when you're on your own that trouble begins, and when he's so much older than you —'

'Mother, we didn't do anything. We just talked. They don't do that at the youth club, you know!'

Mrs Roberts looked a little reassured, but other things were still worrying her. 'He's making use of you,' she said. 'He comes snooping around, and he can't get anything out of me, so he tries to find out what you know.'

'He told me a lot about Dad.'

'I don't want to hear it.'

'He said that Dad went to Germany to examine some gas shells. Did you know that?'

'I never knew anything about his work, I never expected to.'

'And he had one brought back for analysis.'

'I don't want to hear!'

'And he was working on this when he became ill.'

Mrs Roberts refused to listen, turning away.

'Mother, didn't he ever say anything about it?' Helen implored. 'Listen to me, Mother! When he was ill, didn't he ever talk about it?'

'Helen, it's time you went to bed,' said her mother. 'You came in very late, and you caused me a lot of worry, and I hope you won't do it again.'

'Mother, you aren't going to treat me like a child.' She was determined to have it out with her mother, even if it was hurtful to her. She felt quite calm. 'Mother, I've got to know. Did father ever say anything about why he thought he was ill? Did he ever say anything about Germany? Did he ever say anything about the German gas?'

Her mother looked up. 'Yes,' she said.

'What did he say?'

'The day before he died, in hospital. He was sleeping and I

was sitting by him. He opened his eyes, and he smiled slightly and said, 'It was that German bomb.' Then he shook his head, and closed his eyes again.'

'Mother!'

'I thought he was talking about the wartime, I didn't know it had anything to do with gas.'

'But, Mother, this proves it!' exclaimed Helen. 'He knew it was the German bomb that killed him!'

'I can't see that it makes any difference,' said Mrs Roberts.

'But it does, it makes all the difference! Because if he was killed through his work, you could claim compensation.'

'You don't think they would admit that, do you! Of course they won't!'

'You ought to demand an inquiry.'

'Helen, it would do no good. If there was an inquiry, we should have all the trouble and pain, and it would be for nothing. Because they can't admit – they dare not – that an accident could happen. There aren't accidents at Nancekuke.'

8
A Plan

Helen lay awake half the night, going over in her mind the events of the day and waiting for the moment when she could tell Bill her latest information. To her it seemed the proof that they wanted. This was her father's view of what had happened; he thought he had been poisoned by the gas from the wartime bomb. Helen was absolutely certain now that this was the explanation.

If Bill knew, it might be enough to open an inquiry, even if it was against her mother's wishes. She felt that she could not wait to tell him, she wanted to do so at once. At some time during the night she got up and went past Alison's bed to the window. It was very dark outside; ragged clouds flapped across the sky, with a very little moonlight behind them. She could just make out the roofs of the village street, and the steeple of the church.

Somewhere over there, a little to the left below the steeple, was Bill, lying fast asleep. She was sure that he was not awake, he slipped in easily wherever he went.

She crept back to bed, leaving Bill asleep in the unlit village beneath the wild sky. But he did not leave her thoughts. She kept thinking of something her mother had said. It was true, she knew very little about his personal life, she did not even know whether he was married or not. He was about twenty-four or twenty-five. She wondered if he had a wife.

Eventually she fell into an uneasy sleep.

She woke up feeling excited that she would be seeing him again. On Sundays everyone helped themselves to what they wanted for breakfast. Mrs Roberts was not very good at getting up, and Helen hoped to slip out before she was down.

But it was later than she intended, and her mother and sister were already in the kitchen.

'What time did you come in last night?' asked Alison, spreading butter on her toast as thick as the toast itself.

'Alison,' her mother complained. 'You know we can't afford it!'

'About eleven,' said Helen.

'Naughty!' said Alison, enjoying herself. 'Did Mum give you hell?'

'I did,' interrupted Mrs Roberts. 'And don't think you are going to start the same game. You always come straight home from the youth club.'

'Yes, Mum,' said Alison virtuously. She had scraped off a very little of the butter, and now piled marmalade high on top. 'What were you doing?'

'I went out with Bill Wyatt.'

'Oho!' said Alison. 'Do you fancy him?'

'He's all right,' said Helen. 'He's got ideas.'

'I bet he has!' said Alison, in a way that was far too knowing for her age.

'Very funny!'

'Just because I haven't got a husband to back me up, I hope you two girls aren't going to be silly,' said Mrs Roberts. 'I never thought Helen would behave like that.'

'It's always the quiet ones, Mum,' said Alison biting at last into the toast and marmalade that she had prepared with great care. 'Still waters run deep.'

'Oh, shut up!' said Helen. 'I'm going out.'

'Where are you going, Helen?' asked her mother.

'I'm going to see Bill.'

'No, Helen. You're not to see him again.'

'He wants to go the seal sanctuary – we found an injured seal last night.'

'I thought you were in a coffee bar.'

'We went on the beach afterwards.'

'I suppose you're going to tell him what I told you last night.'

'I must.'

'I don't want you to.'

'I think I must do all I can to get an inquiry.'

'Even if I don't want it.'

'Yes, even if you don't want it.'

'I don't know what you are talking about,' said Alison.

'Helen, you are not going out,' said their mother, trembling. 'You take advantage of the fact that I'm on my own. You are not going out, I forbid it!'

'I'm sorry, Mother. But there are some things which I must decide for myself.'

She was outside *The Miners' Arms* as the church clock struck nine, and was joined shortly afterwards by Bill. They drove down to the seal sanctuary, and on the way she told him that her father had seemed to blame the German gas shell for his illness.

'It could be quite useful,' said Bill. 'Of course, it proves nothing, but we need to file it away with everything else.'

They looked at the seals in their cement pool under the cliffs; those which were most ill were inside kennels. Many of them had burns like the one they had found. They smelt strongly and looked a pathetic sight, with their unhealthy, mangy-looking skins. By contrast a seal that was recovering from pneumonia, and had been in the sanctury for some weeks, looked sleek and well as it dived and swam in the pool. Bill interviewed the keeper. There had never before been so many seals brought in in one week, and the numbers each day were still increasing. Many of them were very young, and a vet had thought they were dying of blood poisoning. The older ones were having convulsions, and most showed burn marks. He could suggest no explanation, but there had never been anything like it before.

The photographer arrived to take pictures of the seals, and then followed them to the cove to see if they could get a photo of a seal washed ashore. There they met the RSPCA man; he had collected three that morning. One of them was the seal they had found the evening before. It was now dead. The RSPCA man had put down another, and one he hoped to save. There were more interviews and photographs, including one of Helen kneeling by the live seal, and phone call to a vet who had examined some of the dead seals. There was also an unsuccessful attempt to contact the Seal Research Unit.

Bill wrote his report in the car, asking Helen for some help though she felt it was not really needed. She admired the speed with which he put it together; it took her hours to write a composition. Then he phoned it in to his paper.

Work was over, and there was time for a drink before he drove back to London. They went to a pub, and before she knew it he was telling Helen to keep in touch and let him know if there were any developments and then she was waving goodbye as the orange sports car accelerated out of the car park. He had gone, and she was left to walk home to all the flatness of a Sunday afternoon. Her mother was not speaking to her. Alison was out riding.

She took Paul for a walk and all the time she was thinking that Bill had gone, and with him all the excitement of a more eventful world, where what you did mattered. She imagined his car hurtling along the roads of southern England towards London. He must be in Devon by now, she thought. He must be on Salisbury Plain. He must be in the built-up area spreading out from London. By the evening she was thinking he must be home.

After that there was nothing she could picture. She had no idea what he might be doing. Sometimes she imagined him writing surrounded by books, sometimes in a newspaper office, sometimes eating in smart restaurants with beautiful girls. What was his life really like?

All she knew about him was that he had been to university, had done some research work on gases because government money had been available for that sort of study, had been sickened by it and had turned to journalism. He had founded Anti-Gas Action.

Sometimes she told herself how stupid she was, to be thinking so much about someone she had only met for two days and about whom she knew so little. 'You must be mad,' she told herself.

But she still thought about him, and when half-term was over and she came home from school and found a large envelope waiting for her, she opened it excitedly. It was unsealed, sent by printed paper rate, so she realised there would be no letter. Inside were leaflets and photostat copies of some of his articles. There was a small printed slip: *With the compliments of the Secretary of AGA.*

For a moment she felt a slight disappointment that he had not even scribbled a message on it. But what did she expect, *Love and Kisses?* That was ridiculous.

She spent all the evening reading this literature, neglecting her homework. It contained what she wanted to know, though some of Bill's articles were too technical for her to follow. She regretted having dropped 'O' level chemistry, perhaps all the formulae would have made more sense if she had continued the subject.

The less technical articles were quite clear and a lot of them were horrifying. She was sickened by the accounts of experiments on animals to show the effects of poison gases. There were some photographs of a man's arm that had been exposed to CS gas. It was blackened and covered with blisters. This was supposed to be a relatively harmless gas. Bill showed how the Ministry of Defence tried to make it acceptable by calling it a 'riot control agent' and 'CS smoke'. But if it could do this to an arm, he asked, what would it do to the lungs? He argued that it should be included in any ban on chemical warfare, that it could cause more damage than had been suggested.

This was so-called safe gas. As for the really deadly ones, the effects they produced were almost too frightening to think about. How could her father have had anything to do with such work?

She absorbed the facts and arguments of the leaflets, much

more easily than she memorised school work. It was a pity you could not take an 'O' level in chemical warfare, she thought. She was beginning to feel that she knew something about it.

But she knew nothing more about the William Wyatt who signed the articles. They were efficient, well-written – and impersonal. They revealed very little about the life of the writer.

For the next drama lesson Colin brought a box of hats, about fifty of them, bowlers, top hats, berets, bonnets, helmets, caps. He tipped them out on the floor of the gym and invited the class to try them on, to fool about, to do anything that came to mind.

They tried to take on the character suggested by the hat, to walk around and meet other characters, and gradually to build up a scene. One group were explorers discovering in the hats the only relics of a lost civilisation; they imagined how these objects could have been used.

Helen was in a group of characters who found themselves in a seaside hotel, wearing strange hats and unable to remember how they got there. It created an odd, menacing sort of world.

Afterwards Michael Launder came up to her. 'Are you going to the bus station?' he asked.

'Yes.' She always had to catch a service bus home if she stayed after school.

He walked along with her.

'It was good today, wasn't it?' said Helen. In the past she had been a bit intimidated by him, he was uncouth and insulting. But she now felt so relaxed after a drama lesson that no one could scare her. 'I like the idea of the hats.'

'It's all right.'

'Is that all?'

'It's ridiculous, sometimes.'

'That's what's so wonderful about it,' said Helen. 'It's good to do ridiculous things that you wouldn't dare do anywhere else. It's like being a child again and playing. You lose your inhibitions, it gives you a feeling of being cleansed.'

He laughed at her. 'If that's what you need.'

'It's what everyone needs.'

'Everyone?'

'You seem to enjoy it. You do it better than anyone else.'

This was what she could not understand about him. He seemed to sneer at it and at the teacher, and yet when he wanted he could do it so well.

'I get something out of it.'

'What have you got against Colin?'

'He's a teacher, he's on the side of authority, but he tries to be on your side. He likes to be called Colin.' Mike spoke with great scorn.

'He's the best teacher I know.'

'He does the same sort of thing every week. It doesn't seem to get anywhere.'

'I don't want it to.'

'That's all right for you.'

'Where do you want it to get?'

'I think we ought to do a play.'

'There's not much time for it.'

'We could aim at some sort of performance.'

'I've got my 'O'levels to repeat.'

'It needn't be a full play.'

'We could suggest it to Colin next week,' she said.

'Think about it, see if you get any ideas. But nothing like a school play!'

'What sort of play?'

'Something different. I wanted them to do Beckett or Pinter for the school play, but the boss wouldn't agree. If we could make up something of our own, something that would really shock them. Something they wouldn't like.'

'I'll think about it,' said Helen.

She had suddenly had an idea. She did not dare say anything about it yet in case it came to nothing. Or if she spoke about it too soon she could ruin it. But she knew what she had to do. It was the moment of creation; afterwards would come all the hard work and uncertainties, but as she walked down the drab road to the bus station she felt inspired. It seemed a wonderful idea.

It had only just come to her, but it really went back to the previous week, when her group decided to do a protest against the drama teacher. She regretted then not having suggested a protest against chemical warfare. Now that she had all Bill's information she saw it as much more than a three-minute drama project. It would be a whole programme. She would call it *GAS*. Ideas for different scenes came rushing into her mind, she felt desperate that she would never be able to remember them all.

They reached the bus station, and she joined the small queue for the bus which took workers in the town back to the village.

'Be seeing you,' said Mike.

'Bye.'

For a moment she watched him walking away across the open space, a tall slouching, long-haired figure. He was another wrecker, more bitter and more ineffectual than Bill. He only played at being a rebel, whereas what Bill said and did really counted. His article in Monday's paper had been given a lot of space on the front page. She had cut it out and put it with the rest of his writings.

Then she returned to her hoard of ideas, feeling they would only survive if she kept inspecting them.

'I'm sorry, Mum, I can't stop,' she called as soon as she entered the house. 'I'm late already, and I've got an enormous amount of work.' She went straight up to the bedroom. She did not want to write a script, but she wanted to get all her ideas down before they vanished.

Mrs Roberts made her take a break for a meal, but she was still writing after Alison had come to bed, complaining that she would never go to sleep with the light on.

9
First Moves

In the past when Helen had had ideas they seemed wonderful for one evening, but by the next morning she usually wondered whatever she had seen in them. However, she woke up on Friday morning still convinced that she could make a protest play out of the material she had on chemical warfare. She saw it as a series of improvised scenes, moving rapidly from one scene to the next. The cast would bring in their own ideas as it went along, but it would have to flow from item to item. They could use songs and poems to link it together; one of the things she had to do during the day was to look up Wilfred Owen's *Dulce et decorum est*.

Gas! Quick boys, quick! An ecstasy of fumbling ...

They might be able to bring that in. There were so many things they could use, if only she could get everyone working together. She needed people who could sing and write and act, electricians and carpenters. She would never be able to organise it all on her own, she needed help. She thought Mike would be the right person.

At school, she made a few inquiries about him before assembly. This was the usual time for exchanging information about boys.

Gillian had the reputation of knowing a lot about the boys' school as she was going steady with one of the sixth-formers. 'Do you know Michael Launder?' she asked her, when she found her in the sixth-form room.

'Oh, him!'

'Do you know anything about him?'

'He always chooses you in the drama class, doesn't he? Are you interested in him?'

'I might be.'

'He's weird. That jumper he wears, it's longer than a dress.'

'Why's he so odd?'

'He's always in trouble. He was sent home at the beginning of term because he came back after the summer holidays with his hair down to his shoulders.'

'He's in the sixth form, isn't he?' She thought that in the sixth form the boys could appear more or less as they liked.

'Yes, but the boss doesn't like them to look too way-out. Though he's afraid of driving them away from school, because he wants to keep his sixth-form numbers up. So it's a battle between them.'

'Mike's hair has grown very long again.'

'Yes, I reckon he's about due to be suspended once more.'

'Isn't it silly!'

'Yes, he ought to get it cut.'

'No, I mean silly making a fuss about how long it is. What does it matter?'

'The boss says he'll never give him a testimonial until he conforms. It's not worth risking your future for a haircut.'

'But if you really couldn't give in —'

'Of course he could if he wanted to!'

Gillian was almost engaged to her Keith, with his short back and sides. Helen felt that she liked Michael Launder rather more than she used to.

All day she thought about her play, going to the school library at break and the town library at lunch time to look for books that might help. She had an anxious feeling all the time; she knew now that the idea was good, and she was worried in case she would not be able to bring it off. It seemed such a responsibility. She had to protect and nurture it, carrying it around inside her.

She was thinking about this on the bus on the way home.

'It's like being pregnant!' she thought; she gave a brief laugh and went on smiling.

'Hey, Sis, you want to watch it!' called Alison. 'You know

what that's a sign of, they'll be taking you away if you aren't careful!'

Helen controlled her smile.

'What's so funny, anyway?'

'I just thought of something.'

Alison shook her head, as though her worst suspicions were confirmed.

The play had to be a success, she thought. It had to be more than just one session at the drama club, it had to be seen and noticed by everyone. It would enable her to say what she felt about her father's death and the way he had been killed. It would hurl defiance at those faceless men who denied her mother compensation. You never saw them, you never knew who they were; when she and Bill had gone to the gates there was only a sense of nothingness beyond them. But they would hear what she had to say.

This was really why it was so important to her. But she had to admit too that she wanted to do it for Bill. She wanted to show him that she could contribute in her own way to his campaign, that she was not insignificant but worth his notice. She supposed she wanted to impress him. Perhaps he would come to see it.

It *had* to succeed.

There was a letter from Bill when she got home. She went up to the bedroom to read it.

Dear Helen,

Many thanks for last weekend's scoop. Did you see how the other papers followed it up? It's been National Seal Week in the British press. But we were first, and I owe it to you.

It should all help to alert the public. Have you persuaded your mother yet? By the way, I hope you received the pamphlets and articles.

Did you know there's going to be a demonstration at Nancekuke on Saturday week (21st November)? I don't know who's organising it, it's not our group. I should like to come down and meet them, but won't be free. Would you do something for me? If I send you a number of membership leaflets, would you distribute them at the demo? We ought to have a local branch down there — would you find out what sort of feeling there is, what sort of people turn out, and send me a report on the whole affair?

Hope I'm not asking too much — I know how busy you are with 'O'levels!'

Sincerely,

Bill Wyatt

Her immediate feeling was one of regret. She wished Bill had been coming to report the demonstration, they could have gone together.

No, she had not persuaded her mother. It was difficult when they were still barely on speaking terms. But she was pleased about the publicity, if more and more people were associating Nancekuke with danger. The only way was to shout loud enough and hope that people would hear. That was what she wanted the drama production to do. The play was the thing.

She liked the idea of taking part in the demonstration. This was what they should be doing as well, not just play acting but demonstrating in earnest. She was surprised she had heard nothing about it, it had not been very well publicised.

She wrote back to Bill, saying she would do what she could. She decided not to mention the play yet, not until it had more definite existence. Then she tried to work out another idea she had had for the play. She wanted to use a shadowgraph; it would make figures distorted in a way which might be very useful if they tried to illustrate the effects of gas. The only room she could use was the living room, because no other room had an electric point, and she tried to fix up a sheet with a table lamp behind it to see what shadows she could get. She had Tom standing behind, telling him to move nearer or further away or to hold out his arms, but the light was not strong enough. She thought if it was properly made it would work well. Then Tom got fed up and the rest of the family wanted to watch television, and she had to leave it.

'Mum, you'll have to take her to a fizzy-therapist, or whatever it is.'

'A psychiatrist, dear,' said Mrs Roberts.

'Yes, that's what she needs,' said Alison. The business with the sheets and the lamp was even more proof. 'She's gone right round the bend.'

Helen decided that she would not be much good at telling the drama group about her idea for a production. She was conscious of her in-between status, neither fifth- nor sixth-former, and it was a special concession that she was in the group at all. Also she always felt uncertain when trying to explain what she thought, especially if it was at all personal. To tell a crowd of sixth-formers what she wanted them to do when they had not even asked her was more than she could face. She had to see Mike before Thursday, and put it all to him; then between them they could get to work on the drama group.

So she wrote him a note, sending it by Gillian and Keith, and she had a reply when Gillian returned for afternoon register on Tuesday. He said he would meet her after school. Helen scribbled a note for her mother to say she would be coming home on the service bus, and gave it to Alison to deliver.

At four o'clock she stayed in the form room for a while, to give Mike time to walk the half mile from the boys' school, and then went out. He was waiting for her opposite the main gates. They went to a coffee bar. It had once been *The Bluebird Café*, and then it became *L'Oiseau Bleu* and the prices went up. They knew it would not be crowded.

Over their coffee, she explained what she had in mind. She started rather diffidently. She found that when you have been thinking a lot about an idea on your own, and then you try to share it with someone else, the whole idea seems to change. You see it from a different point of view, and Helen wondered how it could interest anyone else. She was reluctant to use the word 'gas'; it seemed such a personal obsession, she thought it could only be ridiculous to another person.

But Mike nodded, and kept stirring his coffee round and round, listening intently. From time to time he said, 'Great!'

Helen gained confidence and spoke more and more enthusiastically, her words coming in a rush. Mike had never been one to show much excitement, but once or twice he looked up from his coffee and grinned, probably at the thought of the reception certain scenes would have.

She had gone on to describe individual scenes they could include. 'But I don't want it to be too set. We could just have general ideas, and then work them out. We could improvise all these scenes, and then put them together in the right order. I've written down some things.'

She took out of her satchel her note-pad and some leaflets and books, and piled them on the café table. Mike started to read the notes.

'I've really written too much. It's my idea of how the scenes would work out, but the people doing it would have to work it out their own way.'

She knew what she wanted, but she did not want to impose the way a scene developed on the actors; they had to be free.

'When we've got a scene the way we want it, we would keep it like that, but we wouldn't write a script. It's got to be alive. So that when we do the actual performance we know exactly what we're doing, we aren't making it up then, but we won't have learnt any words.'

Mike was reading her notes; he asked her occasionally to decipher her handwriting. Sometimes he laughed. He was not actually rubbing his hands together, but he seemed satisfied.

'I like this idea of involving the audience,' he said. 'I think this could be developed a lot.'

'Yes, I thought we could have television, with actors playing local inhabitants first of all, and being very complacent about it. "It's a beautiful beach, the sun is shining – it don't worry me at all." '

' "Oi've lived 'ere fifty yer, and oi ain't never smelt no gas!" '

They laughed at their own performances.

'And then the interviewer could go into the audience and ask them their opinion.'

'Great! That ought to get them!'

'You know, we could have a microphone on a boom, and someone else pretending to film it.'

'And then we could really attack them!' said Mike. 'We could have an accident at Nancekuke. Wait a moment, let me get this straight. The audience would be this town, and the wind would be blowing straight from Nancekuke to here. And we would spray water to represent the gas, and if they feel a single drop, then they're dead.'

'We wouldn't want to drench them.'

'Why not? That's nothing to what would happen if there really was an accident at Nancekuke. We've got to make them realise.'

'But not drive them right away.'

'We could play on their nerves. We could make out that the water was really dangerous, an acid or something. And build up the tension with the accident, and then the wind shifts and whoosh! they're all soaked. Hey, perhaps we could put something in the water that would really make it sting!'

'Why do you always want to hurt people?' Helen could never make out how far it was real, and how far an act.

'I don't hurt you, do I?'

'No, but I'm not everyone.'

'All right, just the front row then!' He held an imaginary hose over the table, and swept the area in front of them. 'There they are, the boss and the staff, the mayor and the corporation. Pow! We shoot them out of their seats.'

A couple of fur-coated ladies, taking their afternoon tea after shopping, turned round to look at them, shaking their heads.

Helen laughed at his noisy performance. 'It's no good,' she said.

'It's the theatre of cruelty!'

'No,' said Helen, 'we've got to make them think. And if you insult them too much, they'll just close their minds.'

'You're joking! They could never open their minds. That's all you can do, insult them!'

Helen thought Mike might be a difficult collaborator. 'What about the others?' she asked. 'Do you think they'll agree?'

'They'll be dead against it, a lot of them.'

'You'll try and be diplomatic, won't you?' She could not imagine herself talking to the whole group as she had talked to Mike. She needed him, but he was inclined to antagonise people.

He just smiled.

'Do you think it'll work?' she asked.

'It's great!' said Mike. 'We'll put it on, even if we are the only two in it!'

They discussed how they would suggest it to the rest of the group, and then he walked with her to the bus station.

'Where do you live?' she asked.

He mentioned one of the back streets of the town, and added, 'I live with my dad. My mum walked out on us.'

'That's odd!'

'Oh, not nice people at all.'

'No, I mean, I live with my mum. My dad died.'

'We'll have to get together some time,' he said, 'and cry on each other's shoulder.'

On Thursday they consulted with Colin before the class began, shouting to be heard as the gymnasium rang with cries and the thudding of feet. He called the group together, sitting cross-legged on the floor with Helen on one side and Mike on the other and everyone else sitting around in a semicircle.

Colin said he only wanted to do what they wanted, and the suggestion had been made that they should put on some sort of performance at the end of term. They all agreed with this, though Dixie pointed out that there was not enough time to do a full-length play.

'Helen and Mike have an idea,' Colin said. 'Go ahead, it's all yours.'

Helen made a gesture indicating that Mike would speak, and Mike indicated Helen, who laughed in an embarrassed sort of way and said, 'Well, I thought we could do something about – gas.'

'It sounds like a commercial: High Speed Gas!'

Helen laughed even more, and said, 'No, Nancekuke . . . chemical warfare.' She controlled her nervousness and went on, 'It would be a sort of protest –'

'Oh, no! Not another protest!' complained Gillian.

'Everyone seems to think we want to be protesting all the time!' said Keith. 'I don't want to protest!'

'I had enough last time.'

Mike intervened. 'It needn't be a protest,' he said. 'It could be more of an examination of the subject.' Helen was surprised by his tact. 'It would be a sort of documentary drama on the theme of chemical warfare.'

'But why chemical warfare?'

'Yes, why not something more cheerful?'

'Because it affects us,' said Helen. 'There might be other more important things, but this is the one that's closest to us. We live right next to it.'

'It doesn't bother me.'

'Nor me.'

'It would only worry people, I don't see any point in worrying people.'

'It's not suitable at Christmas time.'

Mike looked at Helen and shrugged, spreading out his hands. 'That's what we're up against,' he said.

'Look, let's give them a chance,' said Colin. 'Could you tell us a bit more about it?'

So Mike explained what they wanted, playing down the

protest and emphasising the poetry and song and improvised scenes. Helen supported him, adding what she could.

'It's all so vague. Exactly what happens in these scenes?'

Helen and Mike looked at each other for help. 'Well,' said Mike, 'Helen had this idea for a scene early on. There are three officials discussing where to build their research station and they look at the map and reject various sites. "I say, old boy, you can't put it here, you know. If anything went wrong, eight million Londoners would be wiped out." "How many would be wiped out if we put it in Cornwall?" "Oh, not nearly so many. And they'd only be Cornishmen." '

'That's satire, that's protest!'

'Well, when you think about it, you can't say much about it without it sounding like protest.'

'Then we should choose another subject.'

'Yes, I think we ought to leave it alone.'

'If it closed down, a lot of local people would be out of work. You don't think about that, a lot of people's lives depend upon it.'

Helen thought this was very ironical.

She thought some people were looking at her in a rather puzzled way; they mostly knew that her father had worked there. There was more talk of suitability, and Christmas was mentioned again.

Colin brought the discussion to a close. He asked how many were in favour of Helen and Mike's proposal. Nine hands went up. There were over twenty who wanted to do a performance, but not about chemical warfare.

They had been defeated, but Helen was immediately thinking that nine of them could meet on other evenings and at weekends. They could still do it.

'I propose we break into two groups,' said Colin. 'Helen and Mike can go off with their group to another room and work out their programme, and the rest of us will stay here and prepare a traditional mummers' play for the end of term. It should be good fun . . .'

Two of the gas faction deserted to the mummers, and they were left with seven.

'It's a good number,' said Helen.

'It's enough,' said Mike.

They marched off at the head of their splinter group to find an empty room. On the way Helen asked Mike if he would come to the demonstration on Saturday, and he said that he would. Helen had the feeling that things were beginning to move.

10
The Demonstration

By lunch time on Saturday she had still not told her mother where she was going that afternoon. She knew that she would not approve, especially when she ought to be revising for the first of her exams the following week. Her mother was upstairs with Paul, who had gone to bed as he seemed to have flu coming, and Mrs Roberts was inclined to fuss when anyone was ill. Helen had laid the table.

'Serve up the soup Helen,' her mother called. 'I won't be long.'

There were two pans on the stove. 'Which do you want, Tom?' she asked. 'Tomato or mushroom?'

'Mushroom,' said Tom.

Helen served Alison and herself with tomato soup, and they all sat down.

Tom filled his bowl with pieces of toast, and took a spoonful.

'Urgh!' he went, spitting it out. 'It's sweet!'

'Don't be silly!'

'You taste it. It's horrible!' Tom had leapt out of his chair, and was dancing behind it in rage.

Helen tried it. It was most peculiar, and very sweet.

'What's the matter now?' asked their mother, coming in.

'It's horrible!' shrieked Tom. 'She's trying to poison me!'

'But that's the sauce for the pudding! Helen, what did you give him that for?'

'Then why is it that colour?' It was creamy fawn, just the colour of mushroom soup.

'It's a white sauce, and I put in a drop of chocolate that Paul left in his bottle.'

'How did you expect me to know?'

'You don't think I would have *two* sorts of soup, do you?'

'I didn't know.'

Alison started to laugh, and one by one the others joined in. Tom's face changed dramatically, and he laughed in a loud, manly way, like his father, 'Ha! Ha ha!' The women's laughter was more of a struggle, and left them feeling helpless. It kept breaking out again, and fading away.

It established a good mood for the meal, which was the slightly odd kind they tended to have: soup followed by steamed chocolate pudding and off-white sauce. It seemed as though the middle had been left out, but as Mrs Roberts said, 'It's what everyone likes.'

As the spasms of laughter died away, Helen thought it was the right moment to tell her mother, unless she went and told her after she had been, and she did not want to do that.

'I'm going to the demonstration at Nancekuke this afternoon,' she said casually.

The atmosphere changed at once; the laughter now seemed far away.

'Why won't you leave it alone?' said her mother.

'I've got to go.'

'You father wouldn't have liked it.'

'I think it's what he wanted. He was turning against it.'

'He never said anything against his work.'

'It killed him. I've got to demonstrate.'

Mrs Roberts shook her head. 'It's very indiscreet of you, Helen. It's all right for someone else, but we're in a special position. I don't want to risk losing my pension.'

'Oh, don't be silly, Mother!' exclaimed Helen. 'You can't lose that, whatever happens. And your pension is daylight robbery. You ought to be getting much more.'

'We can manage all right.'

'Look, Mother, Bill says we ought to appeal. Will you agree? He'll organise it all, you won't have to bother about anything.'

'You don't understand, Helen. You'd have to get lawyers

and that would cost a lot, and then if the appeal is dismissed you've lost all your money.'

'I'm sure Bill's organisation would pay the legal costs.'

'No, you only stand to lose. It's best to be satisfied with what you've got.'

'But it's not right.'

'No, but that's how things are, Helen. And it's no good thinking that you are going to put them right by demonstrating.'

'I shall have done it,' said Helen. 'I shall have satisfied myself.'

She had thought of getting a wreath, and carrying it in the demonstration to lay against the gates, with a card saying *In memory of Thomas Maxwell Roberts, killed by poison gas*. But she was glad now that she had done no more about it. It seemed a rather melodramatic gesture, and such an open use of her father's name would upset her mother. It did seem, too, to be making use of his death. She decided to have nothing in the play directly about him.

A married couple who ran a pottery in the village had arranged to give her a lift, she did not know anyone else locally who was going. She met them in the square, and climbed into the back of their van. She held a bag full of leaflets that Bill had sent. The van smelt of dog-meat and dogs; she could not see out. She remembered the last time she had come along this stretch of the coast road, when she had been with Bill. It was a pity that he would not be there for the demonstration. She wondered what he was doing that made it impossible.

They reached the village from which the demonstration was starting, and parked on the sea-front. There were not very many people about, not nearly so many as Helen had expected. She had thought the car-park would be filled with a great crowd. There were a few groups of young people, some mothers with children in push-chairs, one or two older men in duffel coats. A policeman sat astride his motor-cycle.

Mike was there, wearing some sort of ex-army coat. She gave

him a pile of leaflets, and they went around distributing them. Helen felt like a hostess as she smiled graciously and handed out largesse, with gestures which derived from the drama lessons. Mike gave out his with a scowl on his face. She offered one to the policeman, but he would not take it.

'Oh, please!' she said, trying to charm him.

He took it in a big, gauntleted hand, and pushed it into a pocket.

It was not long before everyone had a leaflet. There were a lot left over, and no spectators to give them to. She stood with Mike.

'Who do you think is organising it?' she asked.

'Nobody,' said Mike.

There were certainly few signs of organisation. You would not have known it was a demonstration except for one or two homemade banners.

'I've got to find out his name.'

'What for?'

She told him a bit about her connection with AGA. An elderly man asked them to sign a petition, and she asked him how the demonstration had come about. He said that he and a few friends had got together and spread the word around; he was proud of the fact that they belonged to no group. 'You'll find all sorts and conditions here,' he said. 'There are Catholics, Quakers, non-believers, Cornish Nationalists, students, artists, housewives. Some are animal lovers who are alarmed by what is happening to the seal population.

'It sounds quite a crowd, said Mike.

The man was mildly interested in AGA, and gave Helen his name and address.

After a while a rather straggling procession moved off, as though on a decision of its own. Helen and Mike joined in. They passed through the village. A few curtains parted at cottage windows, and faces peered out at them, but mostly they were ignored. A few people near the shops went about their own business, very pointedly giving them no attention. 'A load of cranks!' said a shopkeeper at his door.

They began to climb the hill, moving away from the houses. Down below lay the harbour and the grey sea. It was cold and dull, the sort of day on which it never really seems to get light. The procession moved slowly. Helen had given out the leaflets in a mood of gaiety; she had been expecting some sort of release, like that which came from the drama sessions. But there was none of the excitement of stamping out a rhythm, only a rather depressed column going slowly up the hillside.

Mike began to turn his mockery against themselves and their fellow marchers.

At the gates they were met by a reporter and photographer who had gone up by car. The petition was pinned to the notice, and a group stood by it to be photographed. Mike and Helen hung back. People stood around, as though waiting for something to happen.

In the distance behind the fence was the chimney and the complex of buildings; it all looked as deserted as ever.

One of the groups looked more purposeful than the rest. There was some sort of activity going on. They had their heads down, huddled over a box, and one man seemed to be holding a cylinder.

'Come on!' said Mike sarcastically. 'They're going to blow a hole in the fence.'

They moved closer, and saw that the man was blowing up balloons, and two women were attaching labels to them. As they approached, the first bright red balloon rose into the air.

'Oh, Mike, what a beautiful idea!' cried Helen. It seemed to her a perfect comment on what went on at Nancekuke, it was such a gentle and poetic answer to the men who made the gas.

'We shall have to use it in the play. It would make a lovely ending.'

'I'd rather have the water.'

'No, this is *right*!'

A cluster of balloons was released, reds, oranges and yellows; they were bright against the grey moorland and sky.

Some did not rise very well, and everyone ran about tapping them from beneath to get them up. One or two burst on the fence or against gorse bushes. Helen and Mike leapt around trying to keep them high enough until they reached the barbed wire.

It was unfortunate, as Mike later pointed out, that the balloons which survived were going in to Nancekuke, instead of out to warn the world.

They had a lift part of the way home, and walked the rest. Mike said he would come with her and hitch back to the town. On the way they discussed how the demonstration should have been organised, and thought more about their play. Helen told him a lot about her father, how she thought he had died and how her mother had no compensation.

They came to the turning where she had to decide either to pass their old home or take the slightly longer way round. Mike asked why she was hesitating.

'Come on, let's see it!' he said, when she had explained.

It was getting dark as they came down the hillside, and the last light in the sky fell on the front of the house. It was still empty.

'Shall we look around?'

'No,' said Helen. And yet she was surprised how in only a month she had grown used to what she had once thought she would never accept. It seemed much more than a month ago that she had lived there.

When they reached the estate. Mike suggested that they could catch a bus into town and go to the discotheque. Helen said her mother expected her to stay in as she had been out all the afternoon and she had a lot of work to do.

They fixed their next rehearsal for Tuesday after school, and said goodbye. Helen hurried in. She liked Mike all right, but she did not think of him as she thought of Bill. She wanted to get on with her letter to Bill, asking him whether AGA would finance an appeal and sending him a full report on the demonstration, with recommendations for future action. These included her first mention of the protest play.

Rehearsals were going well. Sometimes when Helen tried to stand aside and look critically at what they were doing, she felt alarmed. It all seemed so chaotic, a bunch of kids simply fooling about. They spent a lot of time laughing. It did not seem to be getting anywhere.

Yet underneath she felt quite confident. She knew they were finding out what would work and what would not. It looked a mess, but they were beginning to shape something out of it.

They were not like school play rehearsals. Nobody was giving orders. Nobody said 'Speak up!' or 'Face the audience!' or 'Move to the left!' Everyone did what he or she felt like doing, and everyone had an equal say about it afterwards. If any teachers had been there they would have said it was disorganised. And yet it worked.

They met for rehearsals in the boys' school, using the scouts' hut. The girls did not want it known that they were giving so much time to drama. They were sure that it would not be approved, especially for Helen.

There were four boys: Mike, Dixie, who played the guitar, Andy, who sometimes sang with him, and Muscles, a big, heavily-built boy who was quite a comedian. The three girls were Helen, Sue, who was in it because Helen was, their old friendship reviving when they were together, and Frances, who had long blonde hair and was very good at movement.

They decided early on that they would all wear sweaters and jeans, and only suggest costume by putting on an officer's cap, a tin helmet, a beret – whatever would make the point immediately, without any loss of time. They would have the hats in a pile onstage, and take the appropriate one when it was needed. There would be no coming and going; they would all go on at the start, and stay there until the end, whether they had a part or not. They wanted to experiment with the shadow-graph, and the boys were preparing one for a later rehearsal.

They took any scene as it occurred to them. At school on Monday the demonstration had been a big joke.

'Ha, ha!' said Gillian. 'The balloons just blew out to sea!'

It was a big joke in the boys' school, too, and in the whole district. It seemed to prove for those who did not demonstrate that they were in the right, that demonstrators were foolish, impractical people.

'That makes no difference,' said Helen. 'It was the gesture.'

'They couldn't even see which way the wind was blowing!'

Their smugness had driven Helen mad. She told Mike about it on Tuesday.

'In the First World War when the British first used gas,' he said, 'they forgot which way the wind was blowing and it came back over their own trenches.'

'We could do that!' said Helen.

So Andy was an officer, Muscles a sergeant and everyone else soldiers. Muscles brought them into line and to attention, and then with a lot of slamming down of heels and a salute in which his arm vibrated like a railway signal, he handed over the parade to Andy.

Andy gave a casual salute, 'Stand easy, men!' He held his hands behind his back and swayed on his toes as he spoke. He put on his upper-class voice. 'Now, chaps, we have here our new secret weapon. It's called gas, G-A-S, gas. And with this new secret weapon we are going to knock Jerry for six.'

'They didn't call them "Jerry" in the first war.'

'What did they call them then?'

'Boche.'

'You can't say "knock the Boche for six!" '

'Why not?'

'It doesn't sound right. Shut up, you've put me off. Where was I?' He struggled back into character. 'Now you chaps are privileged to be the first to use this weapon. Sergeant, hand each man a grenade.'

'How do you know they were grenades?'

'I don't.'

'They were probably shells.'

'It'll be more effective to have hand grenades, and throw them into the audience. Pow!'

'But it's not historically true.'

'That doesn't matter.'

'We could do the firing of the gun in mime.'

'Yes, that would be good. The team passing the shells to each other, loading the gun and firing.'

'It doesn't hit the audience so much.'

'All right, so they're hand grenades.'

Muscles distributed them ceremonially.

'Now, chaps, I want you to lob them against the Jerries.'

The troops started throwing them into the audience.

'Wait a minute, couldn't we have a count-down? It would be more –'

'Try it.'

'Now, chaps, this is an historic moment in the history of warfare. Your bombs have been individually blessed by the padre. When I give the word of command, I want you to throw your grenades. Five ... four ... three ... two ... one ... zero!'

The troops threw again.

'No, Sue, you look as though you're playing tennis! It's a bomb you've got there!'

The boys gave her some demonstrations.

'That should really get them ducking in their seats,' said Mike with satisfaction.

'Give them a few seconds, chaps, and then Jerry'll come running out of his trenches. And then you can mow him down!'

'Very good sir!'

'Look, shouldn't we all be holding guns, ready to fire them into the audience.'

'Yes, and keep like that. Dead silence for a moment. And then Dixie.'

'I can't see them running, sir.'

'Hang on a minute,' said Andy, peering through binoculars

at the audience. 'There's this dashed yellow cloud, I can't see a thing.'

'It's coming nearer, sir!'

'It's right over us!'

'I can't see, I'm choking!'

They all began feeling around them as though they were blind, coughing and spluttering and clawing the air.

'I say, sergeant, I'm afraid I've been a silly.'

'Yes, sir?'

Andy licked a finger and held it up in the air. 'The wind's blowing the wrong way!'

He clasped his chest, and expired.

By now everyone else was on the floor, and the coughing turned to laughter. Everyone was talking at once about the scene.

'We'll have to keep the coughing fairly subdued at the end, so that Andy's last words can be heard.'

'And then we could go from that into Wilfred Owen's poem.'

'It would be a terrific contrast.'

'Yes, and instead of falling down at the end, we double up, and then we're right into the first line of the poem: *"Bent double, like old beggars under sacks. . . ."* '

'Great!'

11
Act of Betrayal

On the following morning was the first of the examinations. Helen did not feel too bothered about it, as they started with English Language. There was nothing to revise, and she would probably have passed it in the summer if she had not been absent.

At nine o'clock she was outside the examination room, one of a small group shivering partly with the cold and partly with nervousness. At least this time it was not held in the gym, filled with row upon row of desks. Each girl clutched a little plastic bag of pens and pencils.

They shuffled their feet and hugged their arms in tight to keep warm.

A teacher arrived, and they went inside to find their places with their numbers. Helen arranged her things on the desk, put a heading on the answer paper and listened to the instructions as they were read. The question papers were handed out in silence. The only sounds were the rustling of paper and the teacher's footsteps.

She had not felt particularly anxious before, but now her heart was pounding.

'Open your paper and begin.'

The first paper was the composition. She read through the list of subjects, and wondered what Bill would think of them. One was a verse from W.H. Auden, describing the sea meeting the land and the sound of waves going back over pebbles. They were asked to write about the feelings and thoughts it inspired. For Helen it immediately recalled the evening they had found the seal. This, she knew, was what she had to write about.

It came very easily. She found that working on the play might have prevented her from learning facts off by heart for other subjects, but it was a great help here, because ideas and words seemed to flow. She could tap the same source of energy.

At the end she read it through, and was satisfied. She only hoped the examiner could see how good it was! The papers were handed in, they went out and there was a sudden burst of noise as they were free to talk again. They all moaned about the subjects, and how uninteresting they were.

There was a short break, and then they did the comprehension paper. Again she felt quite happy about it, and in the afternoon when they did the English Literature paper, she knew that she might not have done very detailed answers, but at least she was clear about the three set books and had done better than last summer.

After school, they had another rehearsal. Elated by the feeling of having done quite well in the day's exams, Helen expected the play to go on developing as it had at every rehearsal so far. But she was disappointed. Until now they had been carried forward in a rush of ideas and discoveries, but on this Wednesday evening the first impetus seemed to come to a stop.

Helen wanted to practise the scenes with the shadowgraph, but the boys had not got it ready. She had taken from one of Bill's articles a very clinical account of an experiment in which a rabbit was exposed to nerve gas. She wanted this read dispassionately by Mike, while the others mimed the effects of the gas on the rabbit, and either Frances or herself would be behind the screen so that the mime could be shown large.

She felt very frustrated that the screen had not been prepared but she tried to suppress her annoyance. They made a start on the movement. Mike read the passage as she wanted, but the rest of the cast were reluctant. The boys particularly could not be serious; the rabbit twitched and urinated and cowered, and the boys laughed more and more.

Nobody was concentrating. Susan paired off with Andy, and

Frances with Dixie, and Muscles was fooling about. It began to look more like a love-in than a rehearsal.

'Look, if someone comes in, the play will be stopped,' Helen appealed.

'Muscles, go and keep watch!'

'Mike, what can we do?'

'The same as the others,' suggested Mike.

'Oh no! I want to get on with the play.'

'Come on! Why be different?'

'But the play —'

'Forget it for once.'

'It's hopeless! It could be so good, and now it's ruined!'

'It'll be all right. You've been pushing them too hard.'

'I wonder what Colin would do.'

'Oh, he'd give them some exercises. "Roll those shoulders! And one and two and three and four!"'

Helen despaired. The excitement was over. Now the ideas had to be organised and she felt that she would never be able to get them into order.

'I think, Mike, we shall have to drop the idea of a shadowgraph. It would only work in a complete black-out, and we can't be certain of that. I think we shall have to keep the staging absolutely simple, so that we could put it on anywhere. If we had a shadowgraph we would have to have a lot of space behind it, and we could only do it at the end of a hall. But if we keep it simple we could do it on a stage or in the centre of a hall or an ordinary room. We could even do it out of doors.'

'Helen, you're too tensed up about it,' said Mike.

'And it could be just as effective without a screen. We could still do the experiment, but I don't want the boys in it. We'll have just the three girls doing the mime, and you'll still read the description.'

Mike put his arms around her and drew her close to him. 'Stop talking about it,' he said.

'We've got to think about tomorrow's rehearsal, it's no good going on like this. I don't want to ask any help from Colin. I want to do this on our own. So we've got to have a plan for tomorrow, we can't expect it to go on growing on its own any longer.'

'Relax!' Mike murmured, his mouth brushing her face.

'We've got a record player in here, haven't we? We can be certain that's working tomorrow evening?'

'All right, I know you're mad we didn't make the screen. But we aren't all so involved in it as you are, you know.'

'Because I think I'll bring the music of *The Planets*, and we'll try the music for Mars, just moving to it as though it was a gas attack.'

She tried to avoid meeting his mouth with hers.

'Come on, Helen,' Mike pleaded. 'There's no need to take it out on me.'

'Some could be inside their shelters, and the others could be appealing to them, knocking on the doors to get in. There's a part of the music that sounds like that. And then the gas bombs fall.'

'You aren't listening to me, are you?' said Mike. 'All you can think about is your play.'

'Do you know that poem by Peter Porter, *Your Attention Please*? It's as though it was a radio announcement that an atomic attack is on its way and there are two and a quarter minutes left.'

'You're too intense, Helen. You don't listen to what I say. I want to kiss you.'

'It tells people to go to their shelters.'

'I said I want to kiss you.'

'But they mustn't take pets or old people.'

'I want to kiss you.'

'Because they would consume too much air. We could rewrite the beginning of the poem so that it's a warning of a gas attack, and then bring in the music of Mars quietly under the announcement. The early part sounds very ominous, and we could gradually increase the volume, and then when the announcement ends –'

'You aren't listening to me, are you?'

'Yes, I am,' said Helen. 'Have you got a loud-hailer?'

'My God!' said Mike. 'I need one to get through to you.'

'Could you get one for tomorrow? Then you could use it to read *Your Attention Please*. It would sound much more alarming.'

'All I shall use it for is to say Helen Roberts, Helen Roberts, Helen Roberts. I want you, I want you, I want you.'

'But can you get one?'

'Yes, the school has one for Sports Days.'

'Good. We'll try that tomorrow.' She tried to pull away from Mike.

'You have *really* heard what I've been saying, haven't you?' he said. 'You're pretending not to hear, but you've heard it very well.'

'Let me go, Mike!' She looked around the hut. Muscles had gone, and the other two couples were oblivious to everything but themselves.

'You aren't human, Helen Roberts,' he said, dropping her arm and making a gesture of resignation.

Helen spent the evening adapting the Peter Porter poem to make it apply to an attack using chemical weapons, and she wrote a poem of her own on Nancekuke. So she was not very surprised when she could not do the geography and maths exams the next day. They were two subjects she was sure she had failed again.

She now took more control of the rehearsals, instead of letting things arise out of the group. At Thursday's rehearsal they worked with Holst's *Planets*. The music for Mars was too long, but the mood was exactly right, even more so than Helen had remembered. They would use the last five minutes, two and a half minutes as background to the warning announcement, and two and a half minutes on full volume for the attack itself, the appeal to be let into the shelters, the final exposure to nerve gas and death.

To Helen's surprise, everyone worked well, and with complete conviction. There were some moments which were particularly good, when the music seemed to go down and then swell up and they did the same in their movements.

'We must have some lights, and they could go down and up at the same time, music, movement and lights all together.' She turned excitedly to Michael and appealed to him to arrange it. 'Please, Mike!'

'All right,' he said indulgently, as though he was spoiling a child. 'I'll get Jeff and Chris to fix it.'

'Frances, that was lovely, the way your hair was moving and the way you reached out with your hands at the end. Could we all do that and make a pattern with it, all reaching out in the same direction? And then the final collapse. Could we do it once more?'

This time they had a rostrum in the centre, with Frances on that and the others grouped around her. Muscles dropped out, to work the record player.

Then they went back to the poem which led into the movement, Mike speaking it into the loud-hailer.

'How do we go into the poem?' Helen wondered.

'We could have a family listening to the radio,' Susan suggested.

They tried it, and it was terrible.

'We'll have to have a work movement, the sort of thing we've built up with Colin. Everyone doing a factory job, with electronic music in the background, and the movements gradually slowing down as they realise what the announcement says.'

Colin Cordery came in while they were doing this, his own lesson having finished. He watched it through to the end.

'How are you getting on?' he asked. 'It seems very good.'

'Yes, not bad.'

'I'd like to show the two programmes to the school, and the date I've been given is Thursday, 10th December.'

'We'll never be ready in time!'

'It's exactly a fortnight. You can do it, can't you? I thought your play could go first, and then we'd have the mummers' play. It would make a good programme.'

'You haven't seen ours yet!'

'We could repeat it in the evening for parents and friends from both schools.'

Helen's depression was over. She was in a state of excitement about the play, and it was increased by the chance now of a public performance. It was as though the play was a drug, and she was high on it.

'We ought to put all the sound on to one tape,' she told Mike as they were packing away.

'Where are you going to get the electronic music?'

'I don't know. Have you any ideas?'

'We could make up something. Are you doing anything tonight?'

'Well ——' She hesitated. There was French revision to be done, and she was not certain what Mike was going to suggest.

'Let's take all the equipment we can get around to my place. Andy will help.'

'Yes, right.'

They carried a record player and two tape recorders to Andy's car, and six of them piled in. He drove them around to Mike's house, then took the others home.

Mike and Helen set up the equipment in his living room. They had no electronic music for the work sequence, but they experimented with sounds on the radio. Eventually they recorded a foreign station, and played it back with some high-pitched signals on the short waves, and the two combined had a strange effect which was not unlike electronic music. The jerky signals would fit the mechanical work movements very well.

They also wanted a sound to represent gas shells falling. They tried blowing and hissing into the microphone, but there was not enough volume. Mike thought they needed the roar of an engine, but the washing machine did not make the right sound, so he brought in a vacuum cleaner, and by starting that and approaching the microphone to it they got a crescendo of noise.

They were thrilled by the result. Then they put sounds and music together in the right length and sequence on a master tape. This all took a long time, but it was good working together.

'I've missed the last bus,' said Helen.

'Dad'll take you home.'

'When's he coming in?'

'After closing time, I expect.'

'I can't wait that long. I'll start walking.'

'Are you afraid of being along with me?'

'I've been alone with you all evening.'

'No, you haven't,' said Mike. 'You're never alone. You carry your obsession around with you, wherever you go. It's like a third person.'

'Well, thanks for putting up with it.'

'Helen, please stay,' Mike asked directly. 'Please.'

She hesitated. She felt mean, he'd been so good. He'd worked as though it was his obsession as well.

'I'm sorry, Mike.'

Mike walked home with her, leaving a note behind. When they were less than half way, his father came along and picked them up. He took Helen right to her gate. In the house everyone had gone to bed. She was glad to see that her mother was obviously not going to wait up for her any more.

But what made Helen's day was to find a letter from Bill on the kitchen table. She fetched some milk, cheese and biscuits, and an apple, and opened the envelope. She read as she ate.

Dear Helen,

Thanks for your report on the Demo. It was splendid, and I wanted to publish it, but it didn't work out. Still, it was useful to me, and I'm very grateful to you for your trouble. A pity the event itself wasn't more successful!

I've written a very full article about the position your family *is in since your father's death, and how you have had no compensation, even though it's possible that his illness was caused by his work. I think this is the moment to publish it, while people still remember the death of the seals. I don't think we should leave it later than next week, and I think we should follow it up immediately with an appeal to the Ministry. Yes, of course AGA will be responsible for any expenses.*

I know I promised not to print anything without your mother's permission, but in her own interest we must act now. You don't say in your letter whether you have persuaded her to change her mind. Honestly, Helen, this is the moment!

Looking forward to hearing from you,

Sincerely,

Bill

P.S. I hope the play goes well!

The next morning Helen awoke suddenly, with the feeling that it was late. She looked at her watch. It was after eight o'clock, the bus would have gone. She wondered why her mother had not woken them up as usual. Luckily there were no exams, the last two being on Monday and Tuesday, and they were not rehearsing, so she thought that she might as well stay home anyway and revise for Monday's exam. It was French on Monday, and she was counting on that to get her into the sixth form. They had to have three 'O' level passes, and Helen reckoned she had got two, English Language and Literature, out of the four she had taken so far. She did not think she was very likely to pass in history, so it had to be French. She had three days in which she was going to revise.

She hoped in future she would not leave it so late. When she was in the sixth form, and the play was over, she would really work to get 'A' levels and make up for it!

Helen dozed off to sleep again, and when she next looked at her watch it was ten to nine. Alison was still asleep, and there was no sound from the boys. It was quite dark outside.

She got up and went in to her mother, who was asleep with

her head back and her mouth open. Helen switched on the light in the little bedroom. She had hardly seen her mother in the past week, and she was shocked by her appearance. Her mother looked so much older, and her face was drawn and grey.

There was a bottle of tablets by the side of the bed, and a glass of water.

'Mum!' Helen called. 'Wake up!'

Mrs Roberts awoke very gradually from a deep sleep. She looked lost and bewildered.

'Are you all right, Mum?'

It took her a while longer to wake up properly. 'I took some sleeping tablets,' she explained.

'How long have you been having them?'

'I went to the doctor yesterday. I hadn't been very well.'

'I didn't know,' said Helen.

'I hadn't been sleeping at night.'

'Is anything the matter?'

'No, I'll be all right,' said her mother.

Helen felt guilty, she had neglected her mother in recent weeks. 'You stay in bed today, I'll look after you,' she said.

She made tea and toast, but her mother was too tired to eat. She drank the tea, and said she'd sleep off the effects of the tablets.

Helen dressed Paul and got Tom to school, despite his complaints that if his sisters were both having the day off he ought to as well. Alison stayed on in bed. Helen washed up, tidied through the house, and then started to write her letter.

She did not know what to say. She had wanted the truth told all along, and she wanted compensation for her mother as a matter of justice. But she did not know what would be the effect of its publication on her mother at that particular moment. Her mother was ill, she wondered if she was going to have a nervous breakdown. It would not surprise her, after what her mother had been through. And she had not helped her much recently, she supposed. If it was brought back to her by articles in the paper, and perhaps more reporters calling to see her and asking her questions about what she wanted to forget, then it could only be harmful to her. She began to write.

Dear Bill,

Mother is not well. She is very depressed and not sleeping. She hasn't agreed yet to an appeal, and I couldn't ask her at the moment. I think she would be upset by any publicity. Do you think it could wait until she is feeling better?

Yes, the play is going well. There was a time when I thought we weren't going to get the different items to fit together, but now it's beginning to flow from one scene to the next. We are hoping to give a performance on the 10th December. Is there any change of your coming to see it? I'll write again to confirm time and date.

Yours sincerely,
Helen

Between getting meals and keeping Paul happy, she revised French grammar, vocabulary and irregular verbs. She was able to do this sitting at the bottom of her mother's bed, so keeping her company and working at the same time, except that Paul would not leave them alone. The whole weekend passed in this way, and on Monday she thought she had probably got a pass grade in French. Her way into the sixth form ought now to be clear.

She felt very unbothered about the History exam on Tuesday. It was the last paper, and she was accustomed by now to the grim, ritualistic atmosphere of the examination room, and did not let it disturb her. She looked forward to the end of the morning, and the feeling of freedom when all the exams were over.

She answered two questions quite quickly, becoming so involved in them that she had no sense of time passing and forgot where she was. She wondered which question to do next, and glanced around the room. Everyone else was busy writing, heads down over the desks. The teacher supervising the exam was reading a newspaper. Suddenly her attention was caught by the word NANCEKUKE. It was a word she could never ignore, it always stood out on any page. But this was part of a large headline and it was shouting at her. She could not see the whole of it because of the way the paper was folded, but the next word was WORKER.

She began to tremble inside. This must be the article about her family. She could see a photograph which looked like the one of her by the seal on the beach. But Bill must have had her letter last Saturday! Why had he published it when she had asked him to wait?

He must have decided that it would be best. But she had told him her mother was ill, he could not know what effect it might have on her. Perhaps there would be a letter to explain it when she got home.

All her concentration had gone. She wondered if her mother had seen it yet. She wrote another answer, but was thinking all the time about what had happened. She could not understand why Bill had done it, there must be some explanation. She was only waiting to get out of the examination room.

When they could at last go, she asked if she could borrow the newspaper. She glanced it through. Somehow she could not bring herself to read it properly. She could see it was all there, but she felt a great reluctance to read about herself and her family.

The teacher made a stupid remark about her making the headlines, and she felt herself smiling just as stupidly. The other half dozen girls did not know what to say.

She felt cheated, let down. She wanted the truth to be known, but this was not the truth. There were no false statements in it, but when Helen read any parts it seemed as though she was reading about another family, not her own. It was not true in the way that her play would be true.

· The other girls had had more time to take it in. 'It's a shame,' said one. 'It's not right, they ought to pay compensation.' For them it seemed to be true.

Helen had felt vulnerable, personally exposed; gradually she began to feel she could still face other people. She had not realised she would feel like this when she wanted it published. Perhaps it was the unexpectedness of it.

She thought Bill ought to have given her some warning. She thought really he ought to have taken notice of their wishes. She wanted to know what he had to say about it.

But there was no letter at home.

12
Final Rehearsals

Helen found that her mother had heard nothing about the article. She mentioned it casually, playing it down as much as she could. It did not seem to surprise Mrs Roberts. She did not ask to see it, and she did not seem unduly worried.

She was still not well enough to leave the house, so she saw no one to remind her about it. It scarcely registered as an event and the tablets she was having probably contributed to her lack of interest. It was lucky that she was taking them.

'It says that an appeal has been lodged,' said Helen, to make sure that she knew everything.

Mrs Roberts sniffed. 'A lot of good that'll do!' she said.

Helen heard later that it was mentioned on the local television news, and the next day most papers carried brief reports based on Bill's article. No reporters came to the house.

There was now one week before the performance of the play, and with the exams over and the surprise of the article's appearance dying away, Helen could give her whole attention to it.

Dixie had a copy of the paper at the next rehearsal. 'Could we bring this into it?' he asked.

'No,' said Helen.

'Why not?'

'It's too personal. I don't want it to be personal.'

'It's not really, Helen,' said Mike. 'There are other cases as well. I know of at least two men who worked there, and are now so ill they can't work at all. And neither of them gets a pension.'

'Couldn't we have some case histories?' said Andy.

'And between each one Muscles can come on wearing a top hat or a bowler hat or a mayor's chain of office and say "Having visited Nancekuke. I am satisfied that there is absolutely no danger to anyone working there or living in the area!" '

'All right," said Helen. 'As long as you don't use any names.'

'Case history number one,' said Dixie. 'Toxic fitter. Instructed to dismantle a condenser marked "Believed Clean". That night suffered feelings of great heat and convulsions. Has never worked since. No compensation.'

Muscles stepped up on to the box. 'I am perfectly satisfied,' he announced, beaming around, 'that there is no danger to any workers or local inhabitants.'

'Case history number two,' said Andy. 'Toxic fitter. Ordered to work without protective clothing. Has since suffered feelings of intense heat, headaches, partial paralysis. Unable to work. No compensation.'

Muscles took the box again. 'I am perfectly satisfied,' he began, beaming more than ever, 'that there is no danger to anyone at all.'

'Case history number three,' said Helen. 'Research worker. Analysis of a German gas shell. . . .' She faltered, and could not go on. 'You do it for me, Mike.'

'. . . feelings of heat and nervous spasms. Cancer of the blood. Died. No compensation for widow and family.'

'I am perfectly satisfied,' beamed Muscles.

There was a long silence. They all looked at Helen. 'It's up to you,' Mike said.

'Yes, we'll keep it,' she answered.

On Thursday she received the letter she had been expecting for three days, though she would not have been surprised if she had never heard from Bill again. He had used their story and shown no consideration for their feelings. If she thought about it at all, she thought it was mean. But most of the time she did not think about it, she was busy with the play and thinking about that, in

particular the problem of locking the various pieces to fit
together.

By now the article did not seem to matter very much. It had
done her mother no harm. On the whole Mrs Roberts seemed
better, though rather quiet and subdued with the drugs. Helen
still felt slighted by what Bill had done, and he did not seem
quite the hero she had once regarded him, but it did not matter.
The only thing that mattered was the play.

As she opened his letter, she thought that it was going to be
rather amusing to see how he tried to justify himself.

Dear Helen,

*You must have seen the article by now, and I'm sorry, I really
am sorry! You must be thinking the worst of me, and I
probably deserve it. Honestly, Helen, I didn't intend printing it
until your family agreed. But it was taken out of my hands.
Once the editor had seen it he wanted to publish straight away,
and I did all I could to delay it but it wasn't my decision. That's
what the newspaper business is like!*

*I should love to see you again, and explain it to you, it's
much easier face to face. I do hope you will forgive me. Though
I really think in the long run it's for the best, and it would be
great if the appeal succeeds. I'm sorry your mother isn't well,
and hope she's soon feeling better. I wrote the article in what I
believed were her best interests, and those of you all.*

*I shall make every effort to come and see your play. It had
better be good!*

Until next week then,

Bill

P.S. How did you get on with the 'O' levels?

Poor old Bill! She laughed to herself at the way he tied himself
in knots. But she was glad he was coming to the play. After all,
at one time she had wanted to do it because of him. That had
never been totally true, she had also started it to express what
she felt about the way her father had been killed, and this had
been more important. But now she was doing it not for anyone

else but for herself. No, it was not that. She was doing it for itself. It had now a life and energy of its own.

One thing worried her a little. She had told her mother that they were doing a play, but she had not told her anything about the theme. This seemed less than open, but if she knew, it would disturb her more than any newspaper article. 'Your father wouldn't have liked it,' Helen could hear her mother saying. She hoped now for the play to take place without her mother knowing anything about its contents. There was no need to cause her unnecessary anxiety.

They kept adding new items. Andy had found a song in *Oh What a Lovely War*, and he had composed one of his own:

Dulce et decorum est
Pro patria mori
It's the same old story,
It's the same old lie. . . .

It would provide the link from the Owen poem to the next scene.

'We can't add any new material after this week,' said Helen. 'Then we've got the beginning of next week to work on the continuity.'

Quite a lot of it was already in the right sequence, but the final order had still not been decided, and it was impossible to decide when new ideas were still being added. They had to have it ready for a dress rehearsal on Tuesday, when its future would be decided. Colin Cordery would watch it to see if it was good enough to make up a programme with his mummers' play, and the head of the English department at the boys' school would watch it to see if it was suitable. Apparently rumours were circulating about a very revolutionary and subversive work. The cast were delighted about it.

'Is there anything we've left out?' Helen asked. 'This is our last chance.'

'We haven't said anything about transporting the gas along

the A30. A lot of people are disturbed about that.'

'Yes, there was that lorry that overturned on Nancekuke hill. It was carrying acid, but the fire brigade wouldn't go near it, they thought it was gas.'

'They say it always goes in grocery vans.'

'Let's have some workmen loading the van.'

They formed a human chain, passing imaginary containers and stacking them on the box, which became the van.

'Go on, sing something: *"Sugar, sugar, honey, honey"*.'

'Oops! Butterfingers!' said Muscles.

'Steady on, mate! You nearly wiped out the whole of Cornwall then!'

'Right that's the lot then. Pile in!'

Muscles took the wheel.

'Swing about a lot, remember they're Cornish lanes,' Helen instructed. They swung and jolted, and Muscles struggled with the wheel.

'Cor! Be a laugh if we met anyone on these bends!'

He applied his brakes suddenly, and they all shot forward.

'Look out, you silly so-and-so! You aren't on a motorway now!'

He started off again.

'All this holiday traffic! Look at that caravan, let's try and get by.'

Muscles drew out, then pulled desperately on the wheel to get back in again. After a great fight he breathed a sigh of relief. 'Cor! That was a close shave!'

'Now, Mike,' whispered Helen. 'Read out all the towns they go through, with their population – just guess it for now.'

'Bodmin,' said Mike. 'Population ten thousand . . . Launceston, population ten thousand . . . Exeter, population one hundred thousand. . . .'

The van and its crew rattled and bumped on its way. Muscles wiped the sweat from his brow. 'Honiton, population five thousand . . . Ilminster, population five thousand . . . Yeovil, population thirty thousand.'

'Come on, mate! We want to be home for tea. Step on the gas!'

The crew fell about and groaned at the pun, and Muscles, who clasped his hands to his head, had to recover quickly to avoid an accident.

'Shaftesbury, population five thousand ... Salisbury, population fifty thousand . . . Porton Down, population —'

'Porton Down,' interrupted Helen. 'Population, one hundred and fifty-nine scientists, two hundred and eighteen rhesus monkeys, three hundred and sixty-four white mice and four hundred and twenty-nine white rabbits . . . And then we can go straight into the experiment on the rabbit! So we'll have only the boys in the van, Muscles as driver, Dixie as his mate and Andy as the guard in the back. Mike announces the towns from the side.'

'Could I use the loud-hailer again?'

'Yes. As soon as you arrive at Porton Down, go off left.'

'Right, let's get this lot unloaded then! I could do with a cup of tea.'

They piled up the containers in their arms, and staggered off with them, over-balancing and preventing themselves from falling just in time.

'Plenty of sugar to put in it.'

'Don't ad-lib too much. We've got to hear Mike's announcement about the animal population, and as soon as that finishes the girls come on right, Frances on to the box, Susan and me either side, and Mike begins the account of the experiment.'

'Still with the loud-hailer?'

'We don't want to over-do it.'

'But it makes it more impersonal.'

'You like the loud-hailer, don't you?'

'Yes, and you know what I want to say through it.'

'All you're going to say is what's written down here. Now read it!'

The girls did their mime.

'I'm not very happy about the tape,' said Helen, as the rehearsal came to an end.

'Oh, no!' groaned Mike.

'I don't think it's loud enough.'

'I'll ask Jeff,' said Mike, resignedly. 'I expect he can amplify it.'

'He's seeing to the lights?'

'Yes, they'll be ready for the dress rehearsal.' Then seeing that she looked doubtful, 'I promise.'

'We want that film music with the drums for the beginning.'

'Yes, we can use the record for that. It needn't be on the tape.'

'And you can borrow two gas masks?'

'Yes.'

'We've got all the hats we need. And everyone will wear jeans and a black or navy sweater. So that's everything. We should be ready for next week.'

'Yes, that's everything,' said Mike. He shook his head sadly. 'That's everything.'

Over the weekend there was nothing she could do to the play, so she did all she could to help at home. Her mother was up now, but still taking the drugs. Helen worked hard all Saturday, doing the shopping and the housework and minding Paul. She prepared the meals, and after tea started to clear it away.

The table was in a mess. Tom had dug his knife into the tomato sauce bottle, and put it down on the cloth. Then he must have twirled it around, because the sauce was everywhere. Alison had left crusts, crumbs and spilt tea all around her place.

'Alison, you're as messy as Tom,' she said casually, without thinking about it.

They both turned on her.

'Shut up!' shouted Tom.

Alison swore at her.

'Well, you don't do much to help, do you?' said Helen. 'You

might both carry out your own things.'

'I'm not!' said Alison. 'You can do it!'

'Why should I do it?'

'I'm fed up with it!' shouted Alison. 'Leave me alone!'

'But I haven't done anything!'

'Oh no! Only going on all the time about how much you do, and how nobody else does anything.'

'I only said your place was in a mess.'

'So it can be if I want, can't it!' shouted Alison. 'You don't have to tell me what I have to do!'

'You're too goody-goody,' said Tom.

'Well, Helen has helped me a lot today,' said Mrs Roberts.

'You don't know what she's really like, Mother.'

'And she worked very hard at her exam revision.'

'Ha! Ha!' said Alison loudly. 'She hardly revised at all. When you thought she was working she was doing her play.'

'I know she's given a lot of time to that as well.'

'And do you know what it's about?'

'You don't know anything about it,' said Helen.

'Oh yes I do! They're talking about it at school. It's all about Dad and how he was killed by the gas.'

'It's not,' said Helen. 'It's about chemical warfare.'

There was silence. After a while Mrs Roberts said, 'I wish you could leave it alone, Helen.'

'I can't, I've got to do this.'

'It's the sort of thing you can work yourself into a state over, and it doesn't do any good.'

'I think it's better to work it out of yourself. Rather than bottle it up.'

'Is that what you think I've done?'

'Yes.'

Tom turned up the sound of the television and sat in front of it. Now it was winter it seemed to be the only thing he ever did. Alison went to dress for the youth club. Mrs Roberts took Paul on her lap, and she and Helen remained sitting at the table, both suffering, and both unable to say any more.

'I don't like the link after the first poem', said Helen. 'We've got the drums, and the guards marching up and down. The poem ends, and then we've got the First World War scene. I think we need something between the two.'

'And what have you got in mind?' asked Mike smoothly.

'Wait for it!' said Andy.

'Well, I thought the guards could continue marching, and the others join them, all moving like military machines and barking out orders. Like toy soldiers rather, very stiff.'

'The audience would laugh.'

'That wouldn't matter. Then Frances would come in very relaxed and happy, as though she was high on drugs. She would have an aerosol and spray herself with it, and then she'd move amongst the soldiers, very easy and flowing, and she'd spray them, and they'd stop moving like machines and start moving like her. They'd laugh and be happy.'

'It's like laughing gas.'

'Yes, only it has been developed as a weapon. The Americans call it psychogas. When soldiers are sprayed with it they sit down and refuse all orders, they're just happy.'

'That's great!'

'The United Nations ought to have an immense stock of it – they could spray the world regularly.'

'It doesn't do them any harm. Then Frances could spray the audience. She could have an air-freshener, anything that makes a good hissing noise. Psssss! All the cast would then go into the audience, and shake their hands, or touch their hair and their faces.'

Muscles eyes lit up, and he rubbed his hands together. 'I'm going to enjoy this!' he exclaimed.

'All except Muscles,' said Helen.

'Aw! That's not fair!'

'Because you're the sergeant in the next scene. And now you come on in a brisk, military fashion, and you get up on the box and you harangue the troops.

'You what?'

'You call them a miserable lot of lay-abouts, long-haired degenerates, drug addicts. You get them lined up to attention, and hand over to Andy, and we're right into the next scene where he tells them about the new British secret weapon, gas, G-A-S, gas.'

'That's good!' said Susan appreciatively. 'I can see the shape of the whole play now.'

'Well done!' said Mike.

'But it *has* a shape! It starts fairly light, and the types of gas get worse and worse as it goes on, until the whole world is destroyed at the end.'

'Could we try the psychogas scene?' Helen asked. 'After that we'll go through the whole lot.'

'We can't do it without an audience, we've got to touch them.'

'We'll have to make do with one another,' said Mike, eyeing Helen.

'Muscles, the timing is up to you,' said Helen. 'When it's gone on long enough, you come in as the sergeant.'

'Don't worry!' said Muscles. 'If I'm not getting my share, I shall soon put a stop to it!'

The dress rehearsal took place after lessons on Tuesday in the hall of the boys' school. They had not rehearsed the play there before, but this did not matter; they could do it in any space. They had to do it in the centre, with the audience sitting around, because this was the sort of acting area that Colin Cordery wanted for his mummers' play. It had to be in the round.

'Yes, in the round, or against a wall, or on a platform – we'll go anywhere!' said Helen. She could not help feeling a sort of rivalry with Colin, although they were not really competing.

The other group were having the hall on Wednesday for their dress rehearsal. *GAS* had to go first, no doubt, so that there would be time to make alternative arrangements if it was not to be shown for any reason, either political or artistic. If it was not quite good enough, the school probably thought that Colin Cordery could pull it together enough to pass for a public showing.

She felt very possessive about it. It was her child, and she would fight for it like a mother. She would resent any interference from Colin Cordery or anyone else. And if there was any attempt to get them to cut anything out, or tone down any of the scenes, she would withdraw the whole play. She was not going to let anything be altered. It was all or nothing.

The acting area was marked out by a square of chairs, like a boxing ring. There were entrances and exits at each corner, though they only needed two. The rostrum was in position in the centre. Jeff and Chris were on ladders, putting filters over some of the floods. She wanted a green light for certain scenes. They had made a good job of the lighting, it was much better than she had hoped for.

The school had provided two separate rooms for the boys and girls to change in, but they all seemed to end up in the same one. They were all very light-hearted. She hoped they would concentrate during the play. They had to be convinced, they had to do it well! It had to be perfect!

She went through the lighting plot again with Jeff, and then Colin arrived with the senior English Master, an elderly man with a grey beard and gold-rimmed spectacles. They were ready to begin. Jess was ready at the control panel for the lights, Chris was ready with the record player and tape recorder. The cast were far too relaxed, but they said they were ready.

'Good luck!' said Colin.

The hall lights clicked off, a greenish light began to come up on stage, and the music began.

The lights went on again, and the group wandered back into the centre sitting on the box or on the chairs around the ring. It had gone without a hitch, every scene flowing smoothly into the next, every performance absolutely precise and sincere. This was how it was meant to be. If they did not like it, then it could not be because the group had failed to carry out their intentions. Helen felt as though she was throwing down a challenge.

'Splendid!' cried Colin Cordery. 'Absolutely splendid!' He came forward and took their hands, and patted them on the backs. 'A fantastic achievement!'

'What did you think of it, sir?' asked one of the boys.

'I was most impressed,' said the English Master. 'I've never seen you so absorbed in your roles. It was not like a school play at all.'

'Keep it just as it is, don't change a thing!' said Colin. He seemed to be very excited about it.

'You mean we can do it?'

'As far as I'm concerned, it's got to be shown. I'd like the drama advisers to come and see it, it's exactly the sort of thing that ought to be happening. And you went and did it all on your own!'

'We couldn't have done it without you,' said Susan generously.

'No, it was all this shoulder rolling,' said Mike. 'And one, and two, and three . . .'

'Helen was the driving force.'

'It was a group effort,' she murmured. She was determined that Colin Cordery should not take all the credit, but she had to admit that the general approach and some of the particular techniques derived from him. But everyone had contributed.

'Do *you* think we can do it, sir?' Dixie asked the English Master.

'I shall have to discuss it with the Head,' he replied. 'I'm a little worried about the effect on the younger boys. It could be very disturbing for the first-formers.'

'When shall we know?'

'I'll get a decision straight away.'

He went off to see the headmaster, and as soon as he was through the hall door the cast was groaning. 'He's worried about the effect on the first-formers! They'll use that as an excuse. The boss won't want to put it on, he's a military man.

He was in the Air Force in the last war, a wing commander or something. He'll be dead against it.'

'All right, then,' said Helen. 'We don't care. We'll do it in the town.'

'Where?'

'In the streets, anywhere!'

'The police wouldn't allow it.'

'No, but we could get a crowd and perform until they moved us on.'

'Helen, don't do anything rash,' said Colin. 'You won't need to, I'm sure you'll be able to do it here.'

'But I'd *like* to do it in the streets!' said Helen, with a downward sweep of clenched fists.

'Colin, why don't *you* go and persuade the boss?'

'It won't be necessary.' He moved into the centre and spoke lower. 'Look, we all know the boss, and we know he won't like it. Right? But what can he do? If he bans it, he knows you'll go and perform it somewhere else and he can't stop you. All he would have achieved would have been to give you some magnificent publicity. A headmaster can't send a boy home because his hair's too long or too short, without it being in all the papers, so HEAD BANS SCHOOL PLAY would be a gift to them. All he wants is to get it over quietly.'

Colin was more conspiratorial and schoolboyish than the rest of them. He was enjoying this.

'I don't want it smothered,' said Helen. 'I want everyone to hear it.'

'Don't worry, they will! You couldn't do it properly on a street corner, now, could you?'

'I suppose not,' said Helen smiled regretfully. She relished the idea of being strolling players, vagabonds moved on from place to place by the police. It was rather romantic.

The English Master returned. 'The Head says that you may perform your play to the senior school on Thursday morning, and to parents and friends in the evening.'

There were ironic cheers from the boys.

13
The Protest

The school audience, even though they were all boys, had not bothered Helen, but as Thursday evening approached she became more and more nervous. At four o'clock she went straight over to the boys' school and met Mike. She changed into jeans, and they went into the town. She drank some coffee, but could not eat anything.

'It must be stage-fright,' she said miserably. She had never been in a public performance before.

'You'll be all right,' said Mike.

They walked slowly back through the town. It was getting dark, and all the shops were bright with Christmas decorations. In the dressing room the rest of the cast were listening to records and eating sandwiches. The boys had started opening cans of beer. Andy and Dixie were playing cards.

Helen stayed there for a while, but soon felt restless. She took a few sips of beer, but did not like it. Muscles offered her a cigarette, and she refused.

'Let's go somewhere else,' she asked Mike, and they wandered around the school. They went down long corridors, where she read unfamiliar notices to take her mind off the evening, and through empty labs.

They looked into the form room the mummers were using as a dressing room. There were screens across one corner where the girls could change. They found this funny, and Helen laughed hysterically.

'We're much more informal,' they congratulated themselves.

This room seemed to be full of purposeful activity, compared with the idle decadence, the smoking, drinking and card-playing, of their own group. Colin was making-up characters, and people were getting into very elaborate costumes. There was a magnificent dragon's head.

Helen suddenly felt doubtful. 'We aren't using any make-up,' she said.

'We don't need it.'

The preparations for the mummers' play all looked so professional. 'Look at St George's costume!'

'They haven't done any of it themselves,' said Mike. 'Colin's provided it all.'

'Who's next?' called Colin, as one character was finished.

Then Helen saw Gillian and Keith sitting opposite each other at a table covered with books on the far side of the room. In the middle of all this bustle, they were getting on with their homework. Helen had hysterics again.

Their presence and the way they were laughing annoyed the others, and there were shouts for them to clear off.

When they were on their own again, her fear returned, worse than ever. She wished everything could come to a stop. She was trembling all over.

They went back into a laboratory and sat on a bench top with their legs swinging. It was dark except for a little light coming through the windows from the street lamps outside. The dark was reassuring, but she was still terrified.

'I won't be able to go on.'

'You must relax.'

'Mike?'

'Yes.'

'Will you help me to?'

'How?'

'Like Colin does.'

She lay full-length on the bench, with her head close to Mike. He told her to concentrate on the big toe of her right foot, and then to let it drop off. On the next toe, and let it drop off. The next, and the next, and the next. Then the whole foot. And let it drop off. The leg up to the knee. And up to the thigh. And let the whole leg drop off.

And so on, over head and body, until she was relaxed. She lay very still, almost asleep.

'Helen,' Mike whispered. 'It's time to go.'

They returned to the dressing room.

'Thank goodness, you're back!' exclaimed Colin. 'We were going frantic, we thought we'd lost you. I just wanted to say that it's going to be terrific. The audience are crowding in. The drama advisers are there, and one H.M.I.'

'Oh no, please don't tell us, we'd rather not know!'

'And all the local press, and a photographer. So don't be put off by bulbs flashing. And I'm told there's someone from a national paper.

She hoped Bill would not try to see her until it was all over. She could not face him at the moment.

'We've got less than five minutes to go.'

'Please! You keep making it worse!'

'So I'd just like to limber you up.'

Some of the boys groaned.

'Let's do it outside,' called Andy, and they all started to move off, with Colin following. The cold air struck them as they left the building and went into a playground behind the school.

'Brr! It's freezing.'

'Let's shake ourselves out,' said Colin. 'Right arm . . . left arm . . . right leg . . . left leg.' The cold made them shake vigorously.

'Next, reaching up and out as far as you can.'

They all chanted satirically with him,' 'And one, and two, and three, and four . . .'

'Roll those shoulders!'

They rolled for all they were worth.

'Now some deep breathing. In . . . two, three, four. Out . . . two, three, four. And again. Let's have some sounds from deep down in the lungs.'

The night air was filled with ghostly cries. Helen looked up.

The stars were bright, the shape of the school building was outlined against the sky. From inside came the murmur of an audience. A car drew up on the other side. Everything seemed sharp and clear.

The cast continued their moaning, like strange, nocturnal birds. It was beautiful.

'Finally, beat your knees!'

They slapped away at their legs.

'And then SCREAM!'

At the tops of their voices they howled into the night, a cry that must have been heard all the way to Nancekuke. Inside, the audience fell silent, expecting something to happen, and gradually began talking again.

Some of the cast ran once around the playground, and they all burst noisily back into the dressing room. Helen felt nervous, but no longer overwhelmed by it. She wanted to go straight on, and was impatient at any further delay.

Colin gave her hand a squeeze. 'You'll be all right, love,' he said, and returned to his own group.

They moved to the doors of the hall. All the audience were now inside. It looked packed, except for the acting space in the centre. Helen tried not to see any individuals, just a mass of faces, all blurred together. Somewhere amongst them was Bill. And somewhere there were Alison and Tom.

In spite of her intention, she suddenly picked out Alison's red head, probably because Alison intended to be noticed. And next to her, with Tom on the other side, was her mother!

For a moment Helen felt dismayed. Her mother had not intended to come, but if she had it must mean that she felt able to face it. She realised how much she had wanted her mother to see the play, and she was happy that now she was there.

The headmaster took the centre, and the audience fell silent. He made a few introductory remarks. He looked rather unhappy with an audience on all sides, and kept turning around.

'He'll get giddy if he goes on much longer,' said Mike.

But he kept his remarks short and soon sat down. The lights

began to go out. The audience shifted and made themselves comfortable.

Helen took a deep breath, and slipped forward to the rostrum.

All was silent and dark.

Very faintly the drums began to roll, and as they got louder and more insistent the green light began to come up on the rostrum in the middle, and the still figure of Helen. Andy's drum joined the music on the record, beating out a marching rhythm, and the guards moved into the area, patrolling up and down. As the music faded, and the lights came up, Helen spoke out her poem on Nancekuke, fitting it to the beat of the drum and the marching of the men.

She remained on the rostrum with her head hanging, while the guards were joined by the rest of the military automata. Then she jerked into life, and began issuing orders and moving like a clockwork toy to join the others. The audience laughed with some sense of relief after the grim opening.

Frances flowed between them with her aerosol, and as they were sprayed the soldiers began to ignore orders. Two of them started making graceful mirror patterns. One of the machine-like men shouted at them to stand to attention. Then he was sprayed, and the ranting faded away to gentleness.

It was the turn of the audience, and their laughter was tinged with embarrassment as the cast moved amongst them, telling them they were beautiful.

Muscles restored order and discipline, and lined them up on parade for Andy to address. They were issued with their grenades, and flung them into the audience. The gas began creeping back towards them, and they coughed and choked. The officer discovered which way the wind was blowing, and the men, doubled up, felt their way around the rostrum.

Helen spoke the first verse of Wilfred Owen's poem:

'Bent double, like old beggars under sacks,
Knock-kneed, coughing like hags, we cursed through sludge,

Till on the haunting flares we turned our backs
And towards our distant rest began to trudge. . . .'

They dropped out for a rest, sitting on the edge of the box, complaining and asking for fags. Andy became their look out.

An explosion and roar off-stage. *'Gas! GAS! Quick, boys!'* shouted Andy, and the dead-beat figures leapt to life to search for their helmets and fit them on, while Helen continued with the poem.

'— An ecstasy of fumbling,
Fitting the clumsy helmets just in time;
But someone still was yelling out and stumbling
And floundering like a man in fire or lime.'

It was Frances who could not find a mask. She choked and drowned in the 'thick green light, as under a green sea.'

The others lifted the body on to the rostrum, with the head hanging over the edge. The poem told of the wagon they flung him in. They sat on the side as they jolted on their way.

'My friend, you would not tell with such high zest
To children ardent for some desperate glory,
The old Lie: Dulce et decorum est
Pro patria mori.'

'It is sweet and fitting to die for your country,' said one of the soldiers cynically.

'Huh!' said another.

The cast began to croon softly, *'Dulce et decorum est, Pro patria mori.'* It was a twenties or thirties sort of tune, very sweet like a lullaby. *'It's the same old story, It's the same old lie.'*

Dixie sang *'I hate this lousy war, I hate this lousy gas,'* and then as they repeated the lullaby they swung the body off the cart and, still swinging it to the music, carried it by arms and legs out of the hall.

As they went off on one side, Mike leaped on from the other, waving his straw boater hat. The lights came up full, and he did his commercial. 'Come to sunny Cornwall, for fresh air and nerve gas. On the beautiful North Cliffs stands one of the greatest tourist attractions of the county. Admire the slender, elegant lines of the gas factory's chimney. Walk around the perimeter fence and see the friendly dogs behind the barbed wire. Enjoy the cliff walk, open at all times – except when there is smoke coming from the chimney. Bathe in the water that has been used in the process. Hire a gas mask from one of the beach shops. And come to sunny Cornwall, the home of CS and nerve gas.'

The lorry crew came on to load their van. 'Come on, mate, let's make it snappy. Up to Porton Down and back for tea.'

'What's our consignment today, then, Bill?'

'Sixty pounds of nerve gas.'

'How many would that do for, Bill? A thousand?'

'A thousand! Naw! Yer nerve gas does for millions.'

'Right, come on then! Sling some across!'

The gas started on its journey along the A30, and Mike read out the towns it passed through on the route.

This scene moved into the account of the experiment on the rabbit. The lights were dimmed, and the girls did their mime. The moment it ended Mike and Andy came on with hand microphones. They did the prepared interviews with a girl on the beach, a local housewife, and the man who had lived there all his life never smelt no gas.

Then they moved into the audience for the second time, and lights were switched on to them.

'Excuse me, sir, would you mind telling me how you feel about living so close to Nancekuke. Excuse me, madam, would you mind . . .'

'It doesn't bother me,' said one man. 'We need CS gas, and it's got to be produced somewhere.'

'Why do we need CS gas?'

'We need it for riot control. It's done a good job. It's better to fire gas into a crowd than bullets.'

'But don't you think crowds could be controlled with a less

lethal weapon. There's evidence that CS gas in concentration has killed people. And what about nerve gas? How do you feel about that being produced locally?'

'I agree, it's unpleasant. But we need to know what weapons a potential enemy might have, so that we can be prepared.'

'Are you prepared, sir?'

'No, I'm not.'

'Do you have a gas mask and protective clothing?'

'No.'

'Do you have a shelter with a supply of oxygen?'

'No, of course not.'

'Then wouldn't you agree, sir, that it's impossible to prepare against gas attack, and so there is no point in producing experimental quantities.'

'No, because the army can be prepared for it.'

'Are you suggesting, sir, that it's all right for the civilian population to be wiped out as long as the army survives?'

'No, it's possible that only armies would use it, and the civilian population not get involved.'

'Can you seriously believe that's possible, sir?'

'I think it's worth knowing the worst that anyone else can do to you.'

'Thank you very much, sir.'

Andy closed his interview, and the spot-light swung around to Mike on the other side of the hall.

'I've got a lady here who's agreed to be interviewed. Madam, have you ever thought that there might be an accident at Nancekuke?'

'It has crossed my mind, yes.'

'I'm sure it's crossed the mind of everyone who lives in the area. Have you any children, madam?'

'Yes, a boy and a girl.'

'How old are they?'

'The boy's twelve and the girl's eight.'

'Does it worry you that they are growing up close to Nancekuke?'

'No, I can't say that I've thought about it.'

'What would you do if there was an accident at Nancekuke?'

'I don't know really.'

'Have you got a shelter?'

'No.'

'Have you got gas masks for the children?'

A man called out from another part of the hall. 'Look, that's not fair!'

The spotlight swung on to him and Mike moved across.

'Why not, sir?'

'It's a hypothetical question. I don't think it does any good trying to scare people with stories of non-existent dangers. The authorities would take every precaution, they wouldn't allow the slightest risk. There would never be any accident at Nancekuke.'

'Dixie!' said Mike, turning and indicating the figure on the rostrum. The lights focused on him.

'Case history number one,' said Dixie. 'Toxic fitter, Nancekuke. On 22nd December . . .'

And as the three case histories finished all the cast began singing, quietly at first and then getting louder and louder, *Gassed Last Night*, the song from *Oh What a Lovely War*.

As they sang, they moved into their positions for the work movement. The 'electronic' music began, and they began to operate factory machines, computers and typewriters.

'Your attention, please! Your attention, please!' came through the loud-hailer, and some of the audience turned as though wondering whether this was part of the play or a genuine interruption.

The announcement of a gas attack was made, and people were told to go quickly to their shelters. They had stopped work, and stood wondering what to do. They began to run, but fell with the great clashes of sound from the music. The bombs had fallen. They staggered to their feet, and appealed to be taken into the shelters. They hammered to be admitted, but they were not let in. They swayed up and down with the music and the lights. The gas was beginning to take its effect. There was one last appeal as the music rose to its climax, and then they collapsed to the final burst.

Their bodies were slumped across the stage in the green light, and then the cast slipped out during a complete blackout.

It had lasted about half an hour.

The lights came on, the audience applauded, but Helen had decided not to take any curtain calls. They were already back in the dressing room, laughing, congratulating each other, recalling awful moments, experiencing all the sense of release that comes after a performance.

They were not on their own for long. Soon the invasion began. There was a break before the mummers' play, and Colin brought a lot of people backstage and there were congratulations from them all, so many that they began to sound theatrical and false. There were accounts of the audience's reactions, and any hostile ones were recounted with glee.

'Hey, Sue's mum heard someone say that she didn't know what they taught them these days, and no wonder students were so bad!'

Then Helen saw Alison pushing boldly through the crush, dragging their mother along with her.

'What did you think of it, Mum?' Helen asked.

'I thought you did very well, dear,' said Mrs Roberts.

'You didn't mind anything?'

'No, I feel very proud of you.'

'It was great, 'len,' said Alison, giving her sister a nudge.

Someone came in as though arriving with news from the front. 'They're all arguing out there in the hall. There are great debates going on.'

'We started something.'

Suddenly Bill was at the door.

'Fantastic!' He gave her a wink. 'I've got a TV crew on their way, they should be here in half an hour. Can you do it again for them?'

'Oh no!'

'It was just great! I see your mother's here, Helen. Do you think she'd mind if we had a picture?' He had a photographer just behind him, and a bulb flashed, startling everyone. 'And now could we have a family group? Come on, Tom and Alison as well. Mrs Roberts in the centre, talking to the cast. Lovely! Just one more!'

Colin left to limber up his mummers, and the visitors began to leave the dressing room and go back to the hall for the next play.

'I suppose you saw the papers today,' said Bill.

'No.' For the last few days the outside world had not existed for Helen. There had been nothing but the play. It came almost as a surprise that the rest of the world continued.

'There was a short paragraph in most of them. We had a letter from the Ministry yesterday.'

Helen had already guessed the result.

'Yes, they turned down our plea. I thought at least they might have agreed to an inquiry.'

'I'm sorry,' said Helen, more for Bill than for her family.

'I never expected immediate compensation, these things always go through various stages. I shall appeal against their decision next, and eventually we might get the case before an appeal tribunal. But it all takes time. Our best hope is to influence public opinion, and this is where your play is so valuable.'

Bill saw their play quite differently to herself. For him it was a piece of propaganda, for her it was something they had created.

'The next play is about to begin,' a very tall, blonde girl interrupted. She had been standing in the background all the time.

'All right, I'm coming.'

It seemed that Bill had brought her with him.

Now she was alone with Mike in the empty dressing room. All the rest of the cast had gone to see the mummers' play.

'Are you coming?' he asked.

'No, I couldn't.'

'What's the matter?' She was crying. 'Did what the reporter say upset you?'

'No, it's not that, I'm not bothered about compensation.'

She began to sob. Mike stood around helplessly.

'It's all over,' she said, between her sobs.

'But we're doing it again later on.'

'That makes no difference. It's over, as far as I'm concerned.' She put her arms around his neck. 'Oh, Mike,' she sobbed. 'I feel so empty.'

She cried and cried, and he held her tight.

14
The Citadel

The next morning Helen remained in bed. She was utterly exhausted. The feeling of emptiness that she had had after the performance was still with her. She felt drained of all energy. For several weeks she had put the whole of herself into the making of the play, and now that it was over she felt that there was nothing left.

It did not excite her that the production had been filmed and some extracts were going to be shown on the regional television. It had been a great success, she had been applauded and congratulated. It should have been her moment of triumph. And yet she felt that there was something wrong.

She slept fitfully. She kept having long, boring dreams. She tried to keep awake to avoid their monotony, but being awake was hardly any different.

'What's the matter with me, Mum?' she asked, almost in annoyance, as she woke up and found her mother sitting on the bed.

'You're worn out, you need a good sleep,' said her mother.

'I can't sleep properly.'

'You're over-excited.'

Helen wanted to sit up, and her mother plumped up the pillows for her, and took the two from Alison's bed to make an armchair, just as she used to for her father.

There was a tray on the bed, with a pot of tea and a boiled egg and bread and butter cut into 'soldiers'.

'Oh Mum, I'm not a baby!'

'I brought it up earlier, but thought it best to let you sleep.'

'You're spoiling me.'

'Could you eat some breakfast now?'

Helen shook her head, and then felt the hysterical tears of the previous evening returning. She threw her arms around her mother. 'Oh Mum, I'm sorry! I'm sorry, Mum!'

'But whatever for?' asked her mother.

'I shouldn't have done the play. You didn't want me to, and I did it.'

'It doesn't matter.'

'I didn't tell you about it. I was just like Bill.'

'There, there!' Her mother comforted her. 'It was something you had to do, and it was a great success, everybody says so.'

'No, it was a failure,' said Helen suddenly.

'You feel depressed about it now it's all over, that's quite natural. You'll feel quite differently when you've had a good sleep. I'm going to give you one of my tablets.'

Helen took the tablet with some of the tea her mother poured.

'It's just a reaction, you'll be quite all right when you wake up.'

'It was a failure,' said Helen.

Her mother left, and she felt herself getting sleepier and sleepier. She had evaded the issue. She had had to prove that Nancekuke had killed her father. And where had the play got her? It had got some publicity, and Bill said that was all to the good. But he was thinking of what suited him, and she had been thinking of the play, so much so that she had hardly bothered when the appeal failed. It had not brought her a step nearer to carrying out her real task. In fact she had almost forgotten about it altogether.

She drifted away into sleep.

She watched the extracts on television in the evening. It all seemed very much reduced, nothing to make a fuss about. They had cut a lot. When she saw herself on the screen, it was like looking at someone else. There were strands of hair down over her face; she found them annoying, they should have been swept back. Mike looked quite good, though there were not many close-ups. It all seemed rather distant, as though it had very little to do with her, just as Bill's newspaper report had seemed. She was glad when it was over and they went on to another item. She soon went back to bed.

The next morning the other children were at home. Alison complained loudly when their mother came in to the bedroom to see what Helen wanted for breakfast.

'You made me get up and go to school yesterday,' she said to her mother. 'And you let Helen lie in bed!'

'Helen wasn't well.'

'Nor was I, I had a terrible headache.'

'You didn't say so.'

'I did, only you don't listen to me. You only listen to Helen.'

'Well, you can stay in bed today if you like.'

'You wouldn't bring *me* breakfast in bed.'

'I do what I can,' said Mrs Roberts with a sigh. 'For all of you.'

So Helen got up, as she felt much better anyway, and prepared her own breakfast. Alison soon went off riding, followed by Tom on his bicycle. Helen sat over a cup of tea with her mother, who, with Paul on her lap, was grumbling about how the others had left their beds. Helen was waiting for the toast to pop up. They seemed to be back to the usual Saturday morning.

There was a knocking at the door.

'It's too late for post,' said her mother.

'I'll go,' said Helen, as her mother was holding Paul.

She opened the door, and there was a very tall man in a raincoat on the step. She was aware of a car at the gate, with another man in it.

'Miss Roberts?' he asked.

'Yes,' said Helen, puzzled that he should know her name, and then immediately thinking of the television programme, as he could have got it from that.

'Is your mother at home?'

'Yes.'

'Could I have a word with her?'

'What about?' If he was a reporter she would see him herself, but she would keep her mother out of it. She had already made her suffer from this sort of thing much more than she ought to have done.

'I should prefer to talk about it inside,' he said.

Helen kept the door pulled close against her, with the other side of her body against the door post.

'I don't know who you are,' she said. He did not look quite like a reporter, but Bill was the only reporter she knew.

'I'm a security officer,' he said.

'You're what?' said Helen, suddenly feeling the known world of salesmen and Jehovah Witnesses and even reporters slipping away from her.

'Special Branch,' he said.

Helen felt an anxious feeling inside her, as though she had brought more trouble down upon herself and her mother.

'What do you want?'

'May I come in?'

He was a middle-aged, military-looking man in a heavy, belted macintosh. He looked so type-cast for the part that it was ridiculous. She felt a nervous desire to laugh. It was so absurd, a couple of special agents sent to deal with her, a schoolgirl putting the safety of the nation into danger. But it was rather frightening as well. She wondered what they could do to her. She had not broken any law, but perhaps security operated outside the law. Perhaps they would carry her away. . . .

'May I speak to your mother?' he asked politely.

She did not know whether he could insist on coming in or not, but it seemed better to ask him into the hall rather than have her mother meet him at the door. Mrs Roberts came from the kitchen, holding Paul by the hand.

'I'm a security officer,' he repeated.

Her mother looked alarmed.

'Yes?' she said.

'Are you the mother of Helen Roberts?'

'Yes.'

'You weren't on the 'phone, so I drove over. A colleague of your late husband would like to see Helen, if we could fix an interview.'

'What about?'

'He saw the television programme last night.'

'But she hasn't done anything wrong.'

'No, of course not! He would just like to talk it over with her.'

'She couldn't go on her own.'

'You would come with her, of course.'

This would be an ordeal for her mother that Helen would not allow. 'I'm not going!' she said. 'What right has he got?'

'It's nothing official,' the man said. 'It's just an invitation to visit Nancekuke.'

Although he was so polite, it seemed to Helen that there was a hint of menace in his voice. If the 'invitation' were refused, they would be able, somehow, to find ways of enforcing it.

'It seems odd to me,' said Mrs Roberts. 'How do I know you're what you say you are?'

He produced a card. 'Would you like to ring this number and make an appointment? We'll send a car for you.'

'Well, I don't know,' said her mother. 'I suppose we ought to go.'

'Oh really, Mother!' said Helen. 'You always want to do what you are told. You'd hate going there, you know you would. I'll go on my own.'

'No, I won't have you going alone.'

'Then I'll go with Mike.' She turned to the officer. 'I'll only go if Mike can come too.'

'That'll be all right.'

He seemed to know who Mike was, it was rather disturbing. They must have been keeping a record of them all.

'Could we fix a time and date?' he asked. 'When would suit you?'

'Straight away,' she said. Perhaps they only wanted to tell her off, but it could be the chance she needed.

'That's fine.'

Her mother tried to put it off to another day.

'Don't worry, Mum. I'll be all right.'

She put on her duffel coat and black, floppy hat, and the man followed her to the gate. It seemed extraordinary, to be walking down your own garden path with a special agent behind you and another in a car outside. Tom would regret missing this, it was like something out of one of his comics.

He opened the door of the car, and followed her into the back seat. It was rather as though she had been arrested. There were neighbours standing on doorsteps and looking out of windows. I haven't done anything wrong, she told herself, as the large black car moved out of the estate. She looked back, and saw her mother at the gate. She had felt quite confident when she had said goodbye, but now she began to feel uneasy.

The man next to her tried to make conversation, but after a few awkward attempts remained silent.

The car seats were of brown leather, and so deep that she could not see much out of the windows. In front of her the driver's neck was thick and shaven. The bulk of the man pressed against her. She was as good as handcuffed to him.

This is England, she had to keep telling herself. There aren't any secret police. You can't be woken up at dawn and simply disappear and no one ever again dare mention your name. You could not be held without arrest, there was the act of habeas corpus. But she felt as though she was a prisoner, and it was a strange, disturbing journey, with mixed feelings of excitement and dread as to what lay at the end of it.

She was relieved when the car stopped at Mike's house as they had promised. The office accompanied her to the door, as though he was afraid she might escape them. He knocked heavily. Mike came to the door, and looked surprised when he saw them there, and more so when he saw the car.

'Mike, they're taking me to Nancekuke,' she said. 'I want you to come with me.'

'Yeh, of course.'

He fetched his army jacket and locked the door.

Her guard tried to put him into the front seat, but Helen held on to his hand and they sat together in the back. The officer got in alongside the driver, and they moved off again. Helen felt happier now that Mike was there.

'What's going on?' he asked.

'It's the secret service.'

'You must be joking!'

She told him how they had come and collected her.

'But they can't make you!' he said. 'They haven't got any hold over you!'

'I've come of my own free will,' said Helen.

The car slowed down and stopped as they came to the gates, and Helen remembered the last time she had been there, a few weeks ago with Bill. Then it had been dark, and she had felt that she had been throwing down a challenge, knocking at the gates to demand an answer to her question of how her father had died. On that occasion there had been no reply. *Is there anybody there?* Bill had called. And now it seemed that their knocking had been heard, and she was being admitted.

The gates were opened, and the car moved forward into open moorland; the gates closed behind them. She was shut within this secret place, that no one visited and where no one knew for sure what went on. The car sped along the road towards the group of buildings, dominated by the chimney stack. This was the way her father used to come, this was where she believed he had met his death.

She could feel that Mike was as tense as she was. For years they had thought of this place as impenetrable, never to be visited. Now they were inside.

She tried to steel herself; she was not going to be scared into promising anything about her future behaviour. She had to make the accusation and ask the questions, and not let them. This was why she had come.

'Mike, how do you feel?' she whispered.

He squeezed her hand reassuringly.

The car drew up outside a building on the edge of a tarmac landing strip. They were hurried out of the car by the two men, through an entrance and down a corridor. They stopped at a door, the officer knocked and went in, and a moment later they followed.

They had entered what looked like an ordinary office; it might have been a bank manager's. At the window stood a man, his features rather obscured by the light behind him. He came forward; he was about her father's age.

'Helen, thank you for coming!' he said.

'There wasn't much choice, was there?' she replied.

He smiled and held out his hand, which she took automatically. 'Let me have a look at you!' he said. 'You don't look a bit like your father. You know, the last time I saw you, you were so high!'

Helen was rather put out by this conversation, suitable for small children. And if he had not seen her at her father's funeral, she had seen him. She recognised him as one of several strangers that had been in the chapel at the crematorium.

'And this is Michael, is it? I'm sorry your mother couldn't come, Helen. How is she now?'

Helen was suspicious. She glanced around, half expecting the two men to be standing guard behind her, but only Mike was close by.

'Well, there'll be some coffee soon,' he said. 'Let's sit down and have a chat.'

She did not believe that that was what he wanted them for. She was determined to have it out, before the friendly atmosphere he was trying to create smothered her purpose.

'What do you want?' she asked.

'I wanted to see you.'

'Why?'

'Because you're Tom's daughter. He was my colleague, you know.'

'He was my father,' she answered bitterly.

'Helen, I know,' he said. 'I know you're upset.'

'And you killed him!' she accused.

There was a long silence. He looked as though he was going to be angry, and then made an effort to control himself.

'Look, come with me!' he said, with a sort of restrained impatience.

He strode off and they followed, down the corridor and through swing doors into a laboratory. He pushed open another door, and waited for them to go in.

'This was your father's office,' he said.

He started opening drawers and taking out papers.

'These were his notes on the work he was doing.' He thumped them down on the desk.

'And these are the record sheets for the last days he was here. And the accidents list.' He dropped these down.

'And these are the medical reports.' He threw them on top of the pile of evidence.

'I've been through them time and time again,' he said. 'And there's nothing that shows any connection, nothing at all!'

He spoke angrily, as though he was annoyed by the uncertainty of the evidence as well as annoyed by Helen.

'Go on, search! Look around, do what you like! But believe me, I've done all I can to find some clue.'

She picked up a few papers, trying to understand what they were about.

'It can't possibly be proved, one way or the other. It's maddening, but we shall never know.'

He stood by the door and took a pipe out of his jacket pocket. He filled it with tobacco from a pouch, while Helen and Mike looked though the documents. She began to make some sense out of them, and for a moment hoped that she would discover some vital piece of evidence. But as she understood more and more, she realised that there would be nothing that could offer any explanation.

He lit his pipe, sucking the flame into the bowl, and giving her plenty of time.

'Helen,' he began, 'I'm going to talk to you seriously.'

He started pacing up and down, as they remained by the desk.

He told them he always ignored demonstrations and protests, he had only taken notice of theirs because Helen was the daughter of his colleague. He said he was speaking to her as a friend of the family, not officially. He spoke about her father and his friendship for him, of how they had shared the same interests and beliefs. He told her what he thought her father would have said about her attitude and the way she made it public. He knew protest was fashionable, but he would not like a daughter of his own seeking that sort of publicity, and he was sure her father would have felt the same. He prevented any interruptions and arguments. He warned her to drop the subject because she might find it difficult to get into any career she wanted to follow if she had this reputation. He advised her to leave the matter of compensation to the law, and to start thinking about other things.

Helen let him go on, there was nothing else she could do. She had come thinking she was going to demand an admission of guilt, and now she found her resolution ebbing away. She told herself that she was weakening, it was happening just as he wanted. He must be congratulating himself, thinking he knew how to handle her. He must think he was saying just the right things to convince and impress her.

She was not convinced. She was not impressed. And yet all the will to do any more about it drained from her. It was as though her father was releasing her from any further obligation. She only half listened, looking down at the papers on the desk and her father's handwriting, the regular slope of the letters and the maze of carefully written formulae.

'I hope I've made myself clear,' he said eventually, waiting for an answer.

'Yes.'

'Good!' He changed his tone. 'Well, now, let's have some coffee.'

'No, thank you,' said Helen. 'I should like to go.'

She walked out of the room and the laboratory where her father had worked, and where now nothing could be learnt of what had happened to him.

She was glad to be leaving. He gave them a final warning never to say anything about what they had seen or talked about that morning. He seemed to be satisfied, a man who had done his duty.

Then they stood in the wintry sunshine by the side of the car, waiting for the chauffeur. They would go straight to her house, as she knew her mother would be anxious.

'Why did we put up with it?' exclaimed Mike, kicking loose bits of gravel. 'Why didn't we just walk out?'

'We didn't have much chance.'

'He went on as though you were a kid.'

'He thought he had to.'

'But aren't you mad about it?'

'I don't mind,' she said. 'We've been here. I did what I could.' She had taken her task to its limit, right into Nancekuke itself. She could not have done any more.

'And are you free now?' he asked.

'I think so,' she said, and put her hand in his.

The driver came across the tarmac, and they got into the back seat. 'Home, James!' muttered Mike.

The car moved across the moorland. The gates opened and closed for them; Helen knew it was for the last time. She looked out of the back window, and as the car began to descend into the valley, the buildings and chimney of Nancekuke sank lower and lower, until they disappeared into the landscape.